Praise for *Practice D*

"*Practice Dying* is a beautiful meditation on the fear of need, the need for love, and the uncertain nature of faith. Taking us from Dharamsala to New York and back again, Rachel Stolzman Gullo manages to weave a tale both as quiet as breath and as powerful as the blood pumping through our veins." — Miranda Beverly-Whittemore, New York Times bestselling author of *Bittersweet* and *June*

"*Practice Dying* is a remarkably moving story of love in its many forms, familial, spiritual and sensual. Rachel Stolzman Gullo has written a radiant novel that will enchant readers and remind them of the need we all have—to be truly seen by those we love." — Julia Fierro, author of *The Gypsy Moth Summer* and *Cutting Teeth*

"Like the best novels, Rachel Stolzman Gullo's *Practice Dying* deals with life's biggest questions, among them: how do we find the courage to live and love in the face of all our collective suffering? Full of surprise encounters leading to even more surprising developments, this is a novel for seekers, like twins Jamila and David, for whom every day is an urgent and beautiful quest for connection and enlightenment." — Leland Cheuk, author of *The Misadventures of Sulliver Pong* and *Letters From Dinosaurs*

PRACTICE DYING

PRACTICE DYING

a novel

Rachel Stolzman Gullo

Bink Books

Bedazzled Ink Publishing Company • Fairfield, California

978-1-945805-68-4 paperback

Cover Design
by
Isabel Castañares

Bink Books
a division of
Bedazzled Ink Publishing Company
Fairfield, California
http://www.bedazzledink.com

For Bill, Enrico and Gael—nothin' but
big old hearts dancing in my eyes.

Acknowledgments

The members of my writing group, the Exiles, critiqued multiple drafts of this novel over quite a few years; Laura Catherine Brown, Kate Baldus, Anne Hellman White, Kara Krauze, Jennifer Sears, Leland Cheuk, Sharon Guskin, Joseph Keith, Emmeline Chang and Jael Humphries- thank you for your keen eyes and your company in this often lonely pursuit. My old friend, Pablo Bryant read the book at a critical time when I needed a Buddhist and Tibetan fact-checking pass and some fresh motivation and he gave me both. Sharon Guskin illuminated some of the finer points of living a dharma practice that my characters should know. David Levinson Wilk brought to my attention the William Shakespeare quote which became an epigraph. Miranda Beverly-Whittemore, your friendship and steady encouragement throughout this process is something I'll never forget.

C.A. Casey at Bedazzled Ink, was steadfast in all that it takes to turn a manuscript into an actual book—thanks for seeing something worthwhile in these pages. The cover designer, Isabel Castañares, drew forth a vision that was in my head that I couldn't describe or even see myself and she made it into a perfect visual representation of the story.

I'd like to thank my parents and sister, Richard, Marilyn, and Dana—you all have shown enthusiasm beyond what is earned or normal. And with a special thanks to my mother, Marilyn Stolzman, for the text I borrowed from her therapeutic book, *The Healing Power of Grief: The Journey Through Loss to Life* and Laughter. I'm very proud of your bereavement work and writing.

My grandma, Lill, appears as a true-to-life character in these pages, her stories and her spirit. I loved having her with me again by writing her here. His Holiness, the fourteenth Dalai Lama, gave me inspiration for this story. I hope in making him into a fictionalized character, I did him justice. My husband, Bill Gullo, what can I say? You are the only person who can give unequivocal criticism on my writing before you even read it. If there is causality and inciting incidences at work in this book, it is thanks to you. Your care is a constant in my life that I never want to live without. I love you. My boys, Enrico and Gael—when I think about creativity, purpose and making the world a better place, I think of the two of you.

"Practice dying."
   —Plato, on his death bed,
      answering the question of what his
      life taught him.

"We came into this world like brother and brother;
And now let's go hand in hand, not one before another."
      —William Shakespeare

Prologue

WE SLEPT, ONE back against another's chest. Our chins hooked over each other's shoulders and our arms wrapped one another. We pushed to find more space. Sometimes a freed foot or hand would find its own orbit to move about in, for an hour or a day or a week, only to get pinned again, stuck in the tangle. A distant sun sometimes glowed with illumination, and we could see each other, or parts of our own bodies, in silhouette.

We were awakened from our slumber by a rippling current. Our bodies shoved backwards. Our arms rose like wings. The back of one head pushed into the other's face. Startled, we opened our eyes. We saw only in shadows, but we sensed another presence, as delicate as a seahorse. For the first time, we felt fear.

The presence danced lightly in the waters and then swift as an undertow, it vanished. Alone again, we knew something was happening. Our arms treaded slowly through the water, fending off the wake.

We slept hard after the disturbance. A few more weeks rolled by with barely any changing of positions. More light penetrated from outside, more sounds that made an echoing ghostly song. Then there were days where it was harder to sleep because we were pressed for space, so cramped that the slightest movement by one awoke the other, finally leading to our birth into the big world.

Chapter 1

Jamila

FOR THE FIRST eight years of my life I was a *we*. My world and David's world were the same. I didn't foresee that change would come. I didn't know that twins eventually led their own lives.

We were always referred to as "the twins." Our thoughts commingled in our heads before a word was uttered, and we spoke the same words together. Only one of us needed to speak. "We're tired now; we want something to drink; can we play outside?"

So when David began to have thoughts I had no access to, to dream of things I'd never dream of, and to travel to unknown places to receive teachings I'd never learn, I wasn't ready. When David found his calling, he seemed to find a new twin in the world, and I was suddenly without one, blindsided. No longer moving through life in synchronicity with David, I felt I'd lost an eye, turned deaf in one ear.

As we grew up I more-or-less learned how to say "I," but not without moments of utter failure, when I felt like an un-whole person, a half of something. Still, I did have my own existence, a woman who was born a twin, but lived alone.

ON MY LUNCH hour, my mom met me for a birthday lunch. I chose one of the many new restaurants on 5th Avenue in Park Slope that I could walk to from my job. She hurried into the restaurant ten minutes late, carrying a large shopping bag.

"Happy birthday!" Mom kissed and hugged me in my seat, before I could stand up.

She placed the shopping bag at her feet and settled into her chair, making many small adjustments to her clothing and hair. "Did David call you for your birthday?"

"No, but it's only twelve-thirty," I said. I still held out hope that he would call, but our birthday was already over in Asia.

"I have to tell you something. I received an email from the Kirti Monastery. Miraculously, David put me as his emergency contact. He never showed up."

"What does that mean?"

"I don't know. He was supposed to enter the monastery three weeks ago. He still hasn't arrived."

It had become increasingly hard to track David's movements, but still it frightened me that his whereabouts were unknown. I didn't speak of my fears to our mother.

"He probably just stayed longer in Dharamsala." I said.

"Where?"

"Dharamsala. India." I found it unfathomable that she couldn't retain the name of the city where David lived, a place she'd let him visit alone at age fourteen. "He'll get there."

"He was on the plane. They told me that. They don't know where he is."

I felt a chill. "Mom, we should order. They get very busy here."

"Alright, you're not worried." My mother picked up the menu.

She wrinkled her nose when I ordered a burger with cheddar cheese and fries.

"Greasy." She hoisted the shopping bag onto our small table and handed me two unwrapped white boxes. "Happy birthday. I can't believe you two are thirty already."

I opened the boxes to find two stylish, expensive-looking blouses. My mother had more fashion sense than I did and knew it.

"They're really nice. I like them. Thank you, Mom."

"I thought you could wear them to work and out at night."

I wondered if she pictured a more active social life than I actually had. I hardly shared that kind of information with her.

Mom changed the subject. "I hired someone to help Grandma out, since she broke her wrist. Her name is Bethany."

"Why? Grandma's perfectly capable of taking care of herself." I vicariously felt Mom's intrusiveness when it came to Grandma.

"Jamie, Grandma's eighty-nine now. You and I both see her frequently, but that's not enough. She needs someone to check on her every day."

"Every day? That's crazy. So I can't be alone with Grandma anymore?"

"Jamie, please. Bethany will be there for four hours each day. If you go for dinner, you won't even see her."

"Sorry. It's just hard to get used to—Grandma needing help."

For once Mom seemed to hear me. "Yes, it is." She sipped her coffee, and I thought she'd bring up David again.

But instead she asked, "How's your job?" with such enthusiasm that it was as though she'd just remembered that I had a job.

I brightened at the prospect of talking about my work at a center for pregnant and parenting teens.

"There's this amazing girl I've worked with for a few years. She's really important to me. She was—"

"I'm sorry, but do you think I should call the police? I hate to overreact, especially with David. But should we do something?"

I stopped talking and shook my head. Since David and I had grown up and moved out, pretty much whenever my mom and I talked about something personal in my life, it seemed an alarm bell went off in her head —"Jamie's sharing!"—and she would change the topic to David.

"What can the police do? He's in Tibet for Christ's sake."

My burger and her salad were brought to the table. My food looked greasy.

"Okay, okay. But what would you do, Jamie?"

Please eat, I thought, *so we can finish and say goodbye.* But she didn't even seem to notice that our food had arrived.

"You think he's alright?"

"I think he's fine. He goes for months without contact. Why don't you give it a few days? I was telling you something about my job . . . you asked about my job."

"I'm sorry. I'm just worried about David. Please tell me about your job. I'm interested."

Then she turned her attention to her food. Immediately, she needed the waiter for fresh pepper and to "just heat up" her coffee.

"I'm not in the mood anymore."

She picked wilted leaves out of her salad. She would complain to the waiter if she got a good pile of them. I ate my fries four at a time.

"Are you done?"

"Yes, I don't like this restaurant. How was your burger?" We both looked at the sheen on my empty plate and frowned.

THAT NIGHT, I rode the subway into Manhattan with one destination in mind. I got off at Union Square and went directly to my favorite bookstore, the Strand. Many times, David and I had entered the bookstore, parted ways, and met up hours later each having been immersed in different aisles. I walked in and made my way to the back. Standing in the half-light of the poetry section, I read an old favorite of mine, Audre Lorde, who I'd often turned to in times of loneliness. Alone in the Strand on the night of our thirtieth birthday.

At the age of eight, David had left our Upper West Side apartment by himself and walked six blocks to the 92nd Street Y to hear the Dalai Lama speak. That night David explained to our parents and to me that he had seen a flyer advertising that the Dalai Lama was coming to New York and had felt certain he knew him. He had felt like he was supposed to go see the Dalai Lama. Listening to David confess what he'd done and the inexplicable connection he felt to this holy Tibetan man I'd never heard of, sent chills through me. I couldn't remember another time when David brought something important to our parents that I didn't know already.

I looked up from the page I was reading and a man browsing in the aisle immediately caught my attention. His square shoulders made me think of rugby, the striped socks and cleats. His hair was impossibly shiny and black, flopping over a curved forehead, and a feminine brow.

To my surprise, I followed him as he went to the cookbook aisle. He thumbed through a book of Indian food, smiling as he gazed at the pages, seeming to taste what he read.

When he looked in my direction, he seemed to take me in with one long stare. I laughed nervously. He laughed with me, and for a split second I thought maybe I knew him.

"Why are we laughing?" he asked with a strong Indian accent.

I stared at his heavily lashed eyes until I felt myself blush. "Sorry, I'm Jamila."

"Jamila. I'm glad to meet you." He looked at his watch. "I'm late!" He laid his hand on top of mine for an instant. His fingers felt like warm water lapping. As he walked away, he turned back and smiled at me.

I started for the exit, momentarily thinking I was meeting David there to go home. But David was lost, and we didn't share a home anymore. Out of nowhere, this man's voice was suddenly amplified through the bookstore. I thought I was hallucinating. I turned a few corners to find him standing before a microphone, a white-covered cookbook in his hand. An audience of four sat in front of him. My new acquaintance had written a dessert book. I rarely went to nice restaurants and was not much of a cook. Yet I sat in the back row of folding chairs and listened to him talk about studying in London, the spices of his home state in India, and the New York restaurant that had published his recipes in a dessert book. His name was Salam.

After the reading, I waited in line for him to sign my copy of his book.

He opened the cover and turned several pages blindly.

"It's Jamila." My words broke Salam's trance.

"I know. Will you make anything from here?"

"Oh, I don't know. I'll read them."

He stopped on the title page. It read, Sweets of Panjab: Desserts from an Indian Home, and his name was in all capital letters underneath, Salam Mirrani. His gaze landed on these printed words, and I imagined he was marveling at his journey, from his grandmother's kitchen, where he'd spoken of baking his first cakes, to his first jobs in Mumbai restaurants to London, where he had apprenticed, to a bookstore in New York's East Village, where he was currently signing a book of his own recipes for an American woman.

He wrote, "For Jamila. Please. Salam."

My belly tightened. Salam looked at what he'd written before closing the book's cover. He handed me the book without making eye contact.

That night, I sat propped up in bed and stared at Salam's inscription written with a black Sharpie and wondered. I suspected it was an English misuse, but he'd spoken fluently about his book. What was he pleading for?

I'd always loved the railroad rooms of my floor-through apartment, the top floor of a brownstone that I'd moved into with my college roommate after we graduated. Back in New York City, but this time in Park Slope, seemingly far away from the Upper West Side where I was raised, where my parents still lived. When my roommate moved out three years earlier, I decided to live even more frugally and not take another roommate. I turned the front room, the largest, into my bedroom. I put my bed against the windows where I faced the open living room in the middle and could see through an archway to the kitchen, and out the back windows, a long interior view all to myself. I'd found it wasn't too hard to pour myself into my work with pregnant teens, occasionally see old friends, and spend almost no money beyond rent.

With Salam's cookbook full of flavors and ingredients I'd never tasted or even thought to taste, resting open on my raised knees as I looked beyond the circle of lamplight across the dark rooms, I wanted more. I wanted to taste the flavors Salam had pronounced with an accent blended between India and England. I wanted to see the restaurant in Manhattan where he produced those desserts every night for people who sought out experiences and new tastes.

David, where are you, was my final thought before falling asleep.

The following night, I rode the subway into Manhattan to the restaurant where Salam worked. I saw my reflection in the mirror behind the bar, but the woman who was behaving this way was completely unrecognizable to me. I ordered a persimmon dessert. The caramelized fruit dissolved like cotton candy on my tongue. I ate as slowly as possible, putting my fork down between each bite, and even so, I finished before Salam made an appearance.

Just as I was paying the bill, he emerged from the kitchen door. He wore street clothes, not a chef's uniform and appeared ready to head out for the night. He stopped when he saw me.

"Persimmon?" Salam pointed at the traces of glaze on my empty plate.

I nodded. "Very good."

He took off his jacket and laid it over the barstool to my right. "Jamila?"

"Right. Salam," I replied.

He turned to the bartender. "Can we get one of each dessert, minus the persimmon?"

That weekend Salam and I walked across the Brooklyn Bridge together. We met at a small restaurant in Brooklyn Heights, where we filled up on strawberry pancakes and then walked over the bridge, something he hadn't done yet. When we reached City

Hall, Salam guided us north and then west. I didn't ask where we were headed. I listened to his stories of culinary school and life in Mumbai. He described Mumbai as so frenetic that it made New York City seem almost quaint. But Mumbai was a fantastical mix of old world and new. My brother knew Mumbai well, I knew, but it wasn't until I heard it described by Salam that I longed to see it. I released my thoughts of David as I walked beside Salam. *You're not in his thoughts, wherever it is that he walks now.*

Abruptly Salam stopped and said, "Well this is my place. Want to come up?"

It was a non-descript three-story Soho building with a black metal door and three unmarked buzzers. To me it didn't have the homey feeling of Brooklyn. I didn't want to enter the building and start something. I looked across the street and saw a woman walking a large dog. It was a husky of sorts, but my heart skipped a beat, thinking I was seeing a leashed wolf.

I pushed away my apprehension. What would David do? *Start something.*

His apartment seemed impersonal and temporary and I soon discovered why. Salam explained he'd rented a furnished apartment for his one-year stay in New York. I wondered how many months of that year had passed already. Seeing no personal objects of his to add to my knowledge of who he was increased my unease. But when Salam pulled me close and said, "I've wanted to kiss you all day, since we ate desserts at my bar the other night actually. May I kiss you?" I kissed him instead of answering. From there, it couldn't be stopped. The sex was inevitable; I'd guessed that all along. We didn't slow to speak again. Every physical sense was engaged in getting to know Salam. I had to see, hear, smell, and taste who this person was, but most especially touch. He was there to touch.

Afterward, Salam and I lay in bed together, his fingertips tracing circles on my waist.

"Your name is Arabic."

"David and Jamila," I said illogically. "I'm a twin. One Hebrew name, one Arabic–our parents' nod to a peaceful Middle East."

"Salam means *peace* in Arabic."

"Jamila and Salam," I said out loud and immediately wished I could take it back.

"Where's your twin?" Salam asked.

"Tibet." I wasn't going to tell a man I'd just had sex with for the first time that my twin brother was missing. *Was he really missing?* Everything about David felt surreal most of the time.

Salam squinted at me as if this might be a peculiar joke. "Really?"

"He's a Buddhist. Actually, he's a bodhisattva. Very enlightened." I tried to make my words merely playful.

Salam was closely watching my face. "And you? You don't seem like a Buddhist nun." He smiled. "No, seriously, what's that like for you, Jamila?"

I felt seen in a way that I wanted to live in forever.

"David and I haven't been in close contact in the past few years." This was true in some regards, but I never felt great distance from David. And I felt superstitious saying we weren't close when I didn't know where or how he was. I crossed my fingers behind my back, like we would have done as kids.

"And where is your twin?" I asked with a forced laugh. This was a peculiar joke, said without thinking, but there was another question behind the question. For inexplicable reasons, I felt a twin-ness with Salam upon first sight. I was asking if he had that feeling about me. I didn't think there might actually be someone else.

Salam shivered unexpectedly. "I don't have a twin."

"Of course. It was just a joke."

When Salam stood and pulled on his jeans without any underwear underneath, I froze up. Had we gone to a bad place, from one moment to the next? We were merely undressed strangers after all.

But then he leaned down to where I still lay on the bed and kissed me on the lips and my body loosened again.

"Can I make you a cappuccino?" he asked.

"Sure." I stood and pulled my jeans on too, with Salam watching my movements. I grew self-conscious of my naked breasts and reached to cover them with my hands.

"Please don't." Salam curled his fingers into my waistband and pulled me toward him. "Did we just make love?" He smiled shyly. "Maybe we can just do it again real quick."

I held his warm body close and smiled into his chest. "Not real quick," I whispered.

I WAS EXOTIC to Salam, tall and lean, my boyish build, pale skin, his only blue-eyed lover. With his hands on my naked body, he said he felt liberated. He said I was a free American woman, living in my own apartment, coming and going at any time of day. My deep-throated laugh, which he had first noticed at the book signing, all added up to my being an American woman, making him feel light and free too.

Salam should have been exotic to me, too. He had an accent which was new to my ears. His mannerisms and colloquialisms were not ones I could readily interpret. And yet, when I looked into his nearly black eyes, I felt a frightening connection. He was profoundly familiar, the first person who promised or threatened to fit the place that was the missing other half of me. And I began to make us into an impossible we.

I started seeing Salam every Sunday and Monday, his chef's weekends. I took Mondays off from my job so we could be together, a job I hadn't taken or wanted a vacation from in three years. After one of my missed Mondays, my favorite teen, Felicia, asked me if I was in love. I replied no. She shrugged and said, "Just don't give your heart away."

Salam took me on shopping sprees around the city for the ingredients he baked with, places only cooks shopped. We bought live crabs in Chinatown, along with Asian fruits and vegetables I'd never heard of, and spices at the Indian shops in Astoria or the Middle Eastern shops along Atlantic Avenue. We visited the Metropolitan Museum of Art and walked around for half an hour, looked at one painting, and ran out. We went to a movie, and although we didn't talk, we didn't quite listen either. Instead we were distracted by a current of physical attraction that made sitting side-by-side in the dark feel tortuous. We left before the movie had ended.

Physical pleasure was the center of our relationship. We treated sex with reverence, mining each other's bodies for every sensation, every nerve-ending, every response. I was certain my mouth had covered every square inch of his body—I'd seen to it. And every taste increased my appetite. When Salam touched my body, his fingertips communicated, *May I touch you here? What have you and this body seen and done?* My body became conditioned to respond even to his gaze.

THAT FIRST TIME David met the Dalai Lama, His Holiness had given my brother, a mere eight-year-old, a business card with his private phone number written on it. My parents decided it was best to pursue this development that was so important to David. They called the number and a few days later David and Mom went for afternoon tea at the Center for Tibetan Buddhism in Manhattan. My father and I stayed home, playing backgammon and eating leftovers. We barely spoke. It felt like we were waiting to find out who David really was.

"Dad, what are you thinking about?"

"I was thinking I should have gone with them."

"Why didn't you–because of me?"

"You? No. It's my stubborn streak."

Mom looked dazed when they returned. She put her bag down on the table by the front door, pausing to think. David kneeled beside me on the rug, looking at the backgammon game on the coffee table.

Mom approached cautiously as if expecting a challenge. "The Dalai Lama would like to stay in touch with David."

"Stay in touch? How?" Dad asked.

"David can write him and call him."

"Dad, I can meditate," David said. "It's like daydreaming until you're not thinking about anything. I've already been doing it for years."

I had seen David sitting on the floor in his room with his back very straight and his eyes closed, sleeping sitting up. And he also stretched his body into yoga poses he had looked up in a book. When I caught sight of him through his cracked door, arms windmilling from one position to another, or legs lunging into place, he looked very . . . right.

But this was news to my parents. They were both psychologists, but that didn't help them understand a child who discovered a spiritual calling. Our family was Jewish but also firmly atheist; God was a non-issue. At that age, I had not yet asked any of these kinds of questions. What was happening to my twin was only happening to him.

THE LONGER I dated Salam, the more adamantly I pushed away my concern about where David was. I didn't think he was truly lost in the Himalayan Mountains. He was not an unhinged youth in the wilderness, but he felt newly severed, in the same way I'd felt amputated when he first followed the path of the bodhisattva. Memories and stories about David lingered on my lips as things I longed to share with Salam, but I was too afraid to share them.

One late summer Saturday afternoon I packed my bag for my usual overnight at Salam's place. I called him while packing.

"Should I pick up groceries on my way over?" I asked.

"I don't think I can see you tonight. I'm exhausted from the week, very run down."

At that moment, I became brutally aware that I had come to expect his weekends.

"Sure," I said, too loudly. "I hadn't meant to assume."

"I haven't been taking care of myself and it's caught up to me."

I didn't know what that meant. Since when had he not been taking care of himself?

"Okay. Well, get some good rest. We can talk tomorrow," I said hopefully.

The call ended stiffly. I almost called him right back but didn't let myself. Salam and I usually didn't speak from Tuesday to Saturday but just sent a few texts a day, small flirty jokes. I scrolled through my texts and realized that his responses had been tepid all week, and each exchange was initiated by me.

I had a sudden desire to invite him to my grandmother's. My grandma lived in an apartment on the Lower East Side, where she'd lived for sixty years and raised my mother. I went to see Grandma every week. She often introduced into our conversation how much she wanted me to meet the right person and get married, as in, "Find a man who loves children and marry him."

I would have liked to bring Salam to Grandma's apartment and show him the tins full of old buttons, the vintage toys still in boxes, the Pearl Harbor and D-Day newspapers. I wanted him to taste Grandma's vegetable-and-barley soup with fistfuls of dill and admire her folk-art needlepoint pillows. I'd have liked for him to see this other side of me, which was maybe my truest self, Lill's granddaughter.

I also painfully realized that I wanted to introduce Salam to Grandma as my fiancé. *Grandma, this is Salam—we are getting married.* She would embrace him with her eyes closed. He would have to stoop over to hug her, and looking over her head, he'd wink at me. Some deep intuition told me I would never be introducing Salam to Grandma.

On Sunday, I rushed to a matinee screening to avoid staring at my phone. At the end of the movie, I looked for any missed texts or a call from Salam. There were none. I stayed in my seat breathing shallowly. I lay my head back and let the tears flow from the corners of my eyes into my hair. There was nowhere I had to be; no one looking for me. The solitude I'd learned to live with was made unbearable from the time I'd spent with Salam.

I left the theater, trying not to make eye contact with any of the couples or groups of friends walking out into the bright day. I stepped into a small grocery store and bought a sad-looking chicken pot pie for dinner, the kind of thing I frequently ate before I met Salam. *Damn him,* I thought. Why did I want to marry him? I had never wanted to marry anyone before. He didn't throw out old newspapers. He had a mildewed shower curtain. His leather shoes had square toes. He didn't cuddle long enough after sex.

I didn't call Salam, and he didn't call me that entire weekend. As I got dressed for work Monday morning I told myself I wanted to be with my teens in the dedicated, unhindered way I'd loved work before meeting Salam. I'd neglected these girls who meant so much to me, calling in on too many Mondays to share Salam's day off with him.

I spent a couple hours at my desk, pulling together activities for the next few weeks, catching up with new fervor. A midwife was visiting us that day to conduct a childbirth class with the girls. This was normally one of my favorite sessions, but I compulsively checked my cell phone during group, looking at my screen every three or four minutes and seeing no activity at all. I felt mounting shock and dread that Salam and I had gone silent.

I suffered through the group for nearly an hour, barely taking in the discussion, until the midwife asked each girl to choose a partner to practice contraction breathing with. Felicia was in group, and we looked at each other. She had been only fifteen when I first met her and not yet pregnant. She had arrived at the center one day, a petite and clearly determined girl, her hair pulled back in a ponytail so tight it tugged at her temples. She had a wandering eye. She asked me if I could help her to not get pregnant like her mom and sisters all had. Nearly two years later, she did get pregnant—a development I'd wept over—but she was still going to school.

Felicia grabbed my hand before another girl could claim me. I squeezed her hand. *Bring me back,* I thought, *please.*

The paired girls took turns being the mother in labor and then switched. Felicia got to play that role the whole time. She leaned back against the wall, her knees bent and open. I kneeled between her legs and held her hands. Felicia kept her gaze on the midwife, who circled around the room, breathing in and out with exaggeration. Felicia also inhaled deeply through her nose and blew her breath out slowly through her mouth. The midwife paused to watch her through a few breaths.

"Good, lovely deep breathing."

Felicia blinked to refocus her wandering eye and looked at me.

"Good," I whispered, my eyes filling with tears.

Chapter 2

David

AS HIS WHEELCHAIR grew smaller, moving further into the distance, my throat tightened with unshed tears. The rejection I'd been trying to stifle for weeks burned brightly. His Holiness had directed me to come here, sent me away from him to study with a new teacher, in a land he could never enter again. I was banished in this country that could never welcome me, fatherless without my teacher. From the moment my plane from Dharamsala had touched down, I resented my reverse exile to Tibet, and I couldn't see why the Dalai Lama himself had done the exiling.

But for the first time since arriving, I felt *bodhicita* mind, awake. I wanted only to follow this man, this man who'd received the same teachings I'd received and so much more, who was a learned monk who had stepped outside of the dharma practice that was surely his very being to try to burn himself to death.

I'd been in Sichuan Province, occupied Tibet, for a week when I first saw him. A week of solitude amongst people. I was never technically alone. I moved through crowds while I ate in noodle shops, or walked the dust roads or strolled through crowded open markets. I was always practicing my Tibetan with shopkeepers and while playing soccer in the dirt streets with children, but always, every hour and every day, feeling alone.

I purchased my own soccer ball so that whenever I felt like playing with kids, the easiest Tibetans to talk to, I could arrive in one of the bustling squares around Kirti Monastery and start kicking my ball around. The children appeared within minutes to run and play with me.

I only peripherally noticed an old man in a wooden wheelchair, coming into the square to shop for rice, oil, a newspaper, a small bar of rose soap wrapped in paper. I imagined him buying the same things I bought.

When a village teenager kicked the soccer ball too hard, I chased after it as it sped toward his wheelchair. My eyes on the ball, I saw his arm reach down, his strong right hand grasp it. I noticed right away in that one deft movement, in his exposed hand and arm that he was my age, not an old man. As he raised himself half upright in the chair, lifting the ball, my eyes travelled up his bent body. His other hand was masked in a glove, the arm covered by a sleeve. I couldn't take my eyes off his face and neck, the one ear that poked out from the hooded jacket he wore.

His whole head was melted wax. The skin shone in the bright sun, so taut that to look at it made me feel a tight pain in my own face. One eye was melted shut. The other nearly the same, but a dark brown iris seared through a slit of melted skin, accusing the world of being the evil place it was.

He threw the soccer ball overhand and it sailed twenty feet through the air straight at me. I caught it at eye level and quickly lowered my arms to not lose sight of him. I knew what he was, which made me think I knew who he was. He was the self-immolator who had not died. He had doused his monk's robes with gasoline and set himself on fire as a political protest against the Chinese occupation. His mission was supposed to have been a suicide mission. He had once been a monk at the Kirti Monastery, the same monastery where I was supposed to report later that very day.

His Holiness and I had spoken of this self-immolator when it happened.

As I watched from a distance, the self-immolator pivoted his wheelchair and with jerky movements propelled himself away from the square into the carts, motorcycles, and donkey traffic of the main road. The children's voices urged me to throw the ball back into our "field." I felt the dusty ball in my hands and smelled the many smells of rural Sichuan: cooking oil, cloves, pine, and the animal fur smell of people who rarely wash themselves.

I threw the ball to the children and slowly approached the newsstand the self-immolator had just left. I dug into my front pocket for fifty yuan and bought the daily paper, which I could barely read. What would the street vendor think of the westerner who was already a curiosity, inquiring about the outlaw, the living taboo, the self-immolator. I didn't care. I was already in the stubborn grip of new purpose.

"Who was that man?" I asked, turning the wheels of a wheelchair. Squatting low as though I were seated, I pushed the imaginary wheels at my side. I even tilted my head to the ground mimicking how the monk held his body. I squinted one eye. "Do you know where he lives?"

The vendor spoke rapidly, with surprise. I couldn't understand everything he said, but I caught the name which I had, in fact, known but forgotten, Lobsang. But there was little else I could gleam from the vendor's hushed speaking. Certainly not what I wanted to know most, where he lived.

I thanked him and rushed into the road in the same direction Lobsang had pushed himself. He had already disappeared from sight.

I did not make my appointment that day to meet my new teacher at the very monastery Lobsang had left. My bond with my teacher, even a new one I hadn't met yet should have been my highest priority. He could have been the path to Lobsang. But this early decision to pursue Lobsang showed just how deeply I was hurt to have been sent there by His Holiness. And this too is the path, I told myself. Seeking Lobsang is the path of the bodhisattva.

I spent the next few days hanging out in the square, hoping that Lobsang would reappear. Eventually I began walking down the road he'd taken the day I saw him. Each day, I walked a bit further, scanning the outposts along the road to see if he were shopping, or eating laping noodles at a street stall, or drinking po ja barley tea at a roadside tea house. But I never saw him, or anyone else in a wheelchair. With each person I passed I asked myself if they knew him, were perhaps his neighbor, relative or friend. I was tempted to say *Lobsang* to each passerby, *"Lobsang, Lobsang, Lobsang,"* until the name elicited a word or gesture of recognition, directions to his home, a way to locate him.

I had first heard of Lobsang two years earlier, at the time he set himself on fire. The Dalai Lama spoke of him only in passing. I was not his confidant about such matters. But quickly, Lobsang's story became known, a tale of horror that ran worldwide through the Tibetan Buddhist community. There had been a rare uprising in Tibet, a political protest, so rare because Tibetans know that peaceful protest is responded to with deadly violence. Over twenty school girls in Ngaba Prefecture in Amdo had raised their voices against the ruling Chinese who had made their culture and religion illegal. These girls had been shot dead by Chinese authorities. A year later, on the third day of the Tibetan New Year, the Chinese authorities refused to allow the *mourning ceremony* to take place. The girls' souls would not be freed to leave their slain bodies. It had not been enough to imprison them in the material world, they would be trapped forever. And this young monk had left the monastery with gasoline-soaked robes and set himself on fire. To die in anguish, with a tortured mind, is to gravely risk your rebirth. As a Buddhist, one of the first things I learned was to approach my own death with calm countenance, with peaceful joy. That alone would lead me into a positive rebirth, capable of enlightenment in the next life. For Lobsang to cause his own violent death was unthinkable. Self-immolation by a monk, made the whole world I knew suddenly make no sense.

My heart thundered in my chest from imagining our next encounter. And although I was thinking of him constantly and seeking him out throughout my day, I didn't know what

I would do if I saw him on the road, or in a tea stall, or in the square. How would I make him feel the same deep connection that I felt?

I felt this inexplicable connection to Lobsang when I saw him in the square. When he threw me the ball and I caught it, and we looked at each other for several minutes, he was immediately important to me. There was no way Lobsang felt the same intensity I was feeling. But I imagined he felt something kindred. Maybe not as constantly, not as obsessively, but I had entered his thoughts since the day we met. He felt a similar curiosity and hope to meet again.

I replaced my feelings of rejection and exile in Tibet with a deep compulsion to find Lobsang, which I imagined as a reunion. Every day, every hour practically, I admonished myself to forget about Lobsang and to follow the Dalai Lama's instructions to study under my next teacher and continue my Dharma training. I'd leave my guest house each morning and walk directly to the monastery gate. I'd stand there like a tethered donkey, chastising myself because I already knew I wouldn't knock on the doors, wouldn't enter. I pleaded with myself to report to my new teacher, one of the necessary advantages I'd been given—a teacher! But my obsession to find Lobsang overwhelmed all other desires and my feet turned around and headed right back to the square. My thoughts clung to the very person and pursuits I begged them not to. The time I waited in the square shrank, until I was entering at one corner, looking left and right and directly heading out the diagonal corner, down the road. Every step out, away from the square, I scouted and searched, my heart working overtime, beating extra beats with every stride, mile after mile.

By the end of another week, I was walking six miles down the road that cut a dusty swath through the bright green hills of Tibet. Then urged by the position of the sun in the sky, or the call of a passing hornbill, or the emptying of my water bottle, I'd turn around and walk the six miles back. Returning to my own local square and guest house was a respite. I was always looking for him, yet in reverse the search became mindless. On that already covered ground, I often lost sight of what I was doing at all. I walked with an empty mind.

Time wore on, and I stopped going to the Kirti monastery gate, and I no longer worried about my missed engagement with my new teacher there. I also didn't think about Lobsang in the same active way. It had just become my occupation to walk to the square and then down the road, half a day out, half a day back. The walking was a meditation practice. My feet drummed a rhythm. I had imagined how I would introduce myself to Lobsang. In my mind, I repeated the simple sentences in Tibetan until my head was empty. I breathed with the beating of my heart. I was living in a meditation. More like a loyal dog than a man, I was continuously looking for his wheelchair, remembering that melted face, one ear bent to the ground, walking and breathing, my attachment unquestioned.

One morning, pulling on the same clothes, I discovered my pants wouldn't stay up. Holding the button-fly clenched in one hand, I walked over to the small mirror above the wash sink. There was a Tibetan man blocking my way. I froze and then laughed at my mistake. The man in the mirror laughed too. I recognized only my blue eyes, but even they registered first as my twin Jamie's eyes, not my own. I was gaunt and brown and my face was creased with new lines from squinting in the hot sun. I had walked a million steps in a couple of weeks. And what did I even eat? *Bhatmas*, roasted soybeans while I walked?

I went to the open-air restaurant next door and for the first time in weeks I eagerly anticipated what I would eat. I sat at one of the wooden picnic tables, the starchy smell of noodles and rice increasing my hunger. I ordered cold drang-thuk noodles and momo dumplings with tea. When I was done, I ordered another plate of the same thing and ate all of that too. Then I walked to the wares market and bought a belt. I cinched it tight, and bought sugared raisins and every kind of bread roll the woman had for my walk. I headed down the road with my provisions.

As I made to turn around midday, in the exact intersection where I had reversed my journey for weeks, I saw Lobsang seated in his wheelchair in front of a card table playing chess, his opponent seated on a wooden crate across from him.

Growing up in New York City, I'd frequently watched people playing chess at the concrete checkerboard tables built into Riverside Park. I drifted toward Lobsang's table, just as I had as a nosy kid. It was acceptable to hover and watch the chess players in New York. It did not break their concentration, in fact, I had rarely even been noticed. The same held true in Tibet. Lobsang and his partner did not acknowledge my presence.

When Lobsang backed his opponent's king into an inescapable checkmate, I spoke.

"Are you Lobsang?"

He shifted to look at me from his bent position. His one stretched eyelid blinked and he nodded his head a fraction closer to his lap.

"My name is David. I'm a practitioner, a Buddhist. I've been looking for you."

Up close, I could see that his neck muscles and skin were fused. Turning his head was virtually impossible. I wondered if Lobsang was in constant pain.

"I came to Tibet to study at Kirti Monastery. I saw you a month ago. I've been wanting to meet you ever since." I stated my memorized speech in Tibetan which I'd repeated to myself for weeks, as though it were a chant.

"Kirti," Lobsang echoed in response. His face did not display expressions in anything like the way I was used to reading a face. It was like trying to interpret the emotions of an elephant. I would have given anything to spend weeks and months around Lobsang until I learned how to read his face. I could see about a third of his one eye, and the most I could gather from that

sliver of eye was that he didn't want to think about the Kirti Monastery.

My heart raced and I felt a maniac's smile coming over me. "I'm so happy I found you. I've been hoping we could spend some time together."

Realizing the impossibility of us talking freely in public, I shrugged sheepishly. But really, I was unconcerned. I felt that by my sheer will we could connect now that I'd found him. Lobsang rotated the wheels of his chair and began to leave. I followed, trying to convey an easygoing friendliness.

"I'll just walk with you a bit, if that's okay."

Lobsang stopped wheeling his chair and turned to face me. He raised his posture by an inch, just like any man rising to his full height. With a constricted mouth, the upper lip like a raised bridge between ragged nostrils and mouth he spoke in a voice that seemed to be the most untouched by fire part of him.

His eye trained on my face, he said, "You have the wrong person. Do not follow me. I do not wish to speak with you." I understood his Tibetan perfectly; I had been dismissed. But, I continued, by his side when he started moving again.

"I know we're strangers right now. But I don't think we're truly strangers. I think we share something very deep, and I just want to find out what it is."

Lobsang struggled as his wheelchair encountered a broken curb. I took hold of the handles on the back of his chair and tilted it backward, hoisting him over the curb, onto flat road. Right away I understood my mistake. Lobsang roughly spun the chair to face me. He snarled; his voice packed with anger that barely registered on his damaged face. Again, I understood perfectly that he was telling me to get the hell away from him. I couldn't help but smile though, because already I could read his face better than before. He turned away and moved quickly along the road.

I was elated anyway. "I'll come look for you again tomorrow! I'm sorry I pushed your chair!" Despite Lobsang's reaction to me, my happiness was unstoppable. I was convinced all we needed was a little time to talk privately.

I followed him at a safe distance, my only goal to discover where he lived, so we could have a proper talk. I couldn't risk it taking weeks to find him again. He turned off the road into a driveway of sorts. I crept along, not wanting to be seen. It was a typical housing compound in rural Sichuan, a small cluster of concrete aluminum-roofed, one or two-room homes. In one of these, lived Lobsang. I turned around to head home. As I walked I took note of every landmark on the road that led to his home, but I didn't need them. I knew exactly where to find him again.

AT AGE EIGHT, Jamie and I were the same height and weight, had the same wavy, brown hair and blue eyes, and wore the same dark-blue parkas. On Saturday afternoons, our mother ran errands around the Upper West Side, with the two of us in tow. At the dry cleaner, green grocer, butcher, wine store, we were often called "the twins," as in "And how are you twins today?" or "Can the twins have a piece of candy?"

Jamie and I liked to hold hands. We were told to hold hands as we crossed the wide avenues of our neighborhood, and we just kept holding.

One Fall Saturday, Jamie and I played one of our wordless games. She poked my shoulder and then pressed her index finger onto the glass of a gumball machine, a red gumball behind the glass. The rainbow game. I had to find something orange to touch, then she had to find yellow, and so on through the rainbow. The gumball machine could get us almost through this entire game. Our mother misunderstood our playing and said, "No candy, kids."

Our last stop that afternoon was the wine store. Just inside the front door there was a low bench covered with real estate listings in booklets. Mom parked Jamie and me there with the groceries and the dry cleaning so she could pick out a couple of bottles for the weekend. The two of us looked at the black-and-white photos of apartments in our neighborhood. We showed each other the features we liked—hidden staircases, bay windows, dumbwaiters. We whispered about rooms we could live in besides our own, the ones we were born in.

Mom returned with the wine she'd just bought. "Help me carry the packages." She handed me two bags of groceries to carry and held out a bundle of pressed shirts on hangers to my sister.

We stepped out of the store. I was in front. Mom was behind me, her hair blowing in the wind, her arms weighed down with packages. Jamie was behind her, the plastic-sheathed shirts almost covering her entire length, almost blocking her view.

A man came running from around the corner and slammed right into me, knocking me flat on the sidewalk. He fell on top of me, his weight pinning me to the ground for a brief moment before he rolled off.

Clapping my chest and back through my parka with his hands, he did a body check. "You're okay."

He sprang back onto his feet and started to run. I raised my head and saw the bottom of his sneaker, saw a red pepper that had escaped from my shopping-bag, roll off the curb.

I heard a car screech around the corner.

Before the man could make the far corner, the car slowed and pulled alongside him. The nose of a gun appeared in the passenger seat window. Jamie kneeled beside me. Mom had hold of both our jackets. She pulled.

"Kids, get up! Now!"

The gun's firing made an orange flash. The bullet must have missed, because after the flash and the boom, the man turned on his heel, still running. I imagined my finger stopping up the gun. I knew a second shot was coming—like listening to music and knowing the next note will fall. Touch the orange, stop the bullet.

Mom was screaming, "Stay down, don't move!" She pushed our heads under her armpits. All I could see was the darkness of her coat.

We heard the second shot. The car shrieked as it pulled away. Fifteen feet from us, the man lay without moving. I still felt the imprint of his hands on my body.

Jamie and I rose like one body and moved toward him.

Mom yelled, "David, Jamila, stop! Come back here, not any closer."

Jamie looked to her and said, "Mama, see if he's alive."

"Stop!" Mom yelled, but she had no choice but to follow her children.

He was young, maybe twenty. His eyes were dark brown, open, and swimming in tears. They flicked left and right.

Jamie pointed at a bullet hole in the breast of his black jacket, it was a clean hole, burnt around the edges, and there wasn't any blood coming from it. Then we leapt backward as a dark red puddle of blood rushed from behind his shoulder, flowed right to the tips of our sneakers.

My mother pulled us into her body. Jamie clasped her around the waist. I craned to see the man's eyes. Did he feel the blood spilling? His eyes went still, locked on the sky above. His lips opened as if he was about to speak.

An ambulance pulled up and paramedics rushed to the dead man. "Back away, back up, now!"

The three of us retreated. I watched the man carefully, expecting something to happen.

Mom said, "David, that's enough."

I was feeling the young man's weight pinning me to the sidewalk, seeing his eyes scan my face for any hurt. And as though it were happening just then, I felt his strong hands clap my chest and back. "You're okay."

The paramedics unzipped his jacket, pressed oxygen to his face, lifted his closed eyelids. That's when I saw his colors leave his body. Fumes of yellow, green, and blue rose almost invisibly through the air. I watched the rippling current of his colors curl and snake away. I pointed skyward at this phenomena, but when I looked at Jamie she wasn't seeing what I was.

You're okay.

We gathered up our packages. Mom in the middle, each of us pinned to her sides, we trudged home.

The dead man's colors escaping his fallen body were a mystery that I couldn't stop puzzling over.

Two weeks later, I was with my parents and Jamie at the 92nd Street Y for family swim when I saw a flyer pinned to the bulletin board by the elevator. On the flyer was a picture of a smiling man, with eyes that shone behind his large eyeglasses. He wore a red and yellow sleeveless shirt, showing his bare arms. He was oddly familiar.

I walked over to get a closer look.

"His Holiness, the Dalai Lama." *The Dalai Lama, the Dalai Lama.* I silently repeated the name over and over, causing a dizzying vibration to rise from my heart through the top of my head.

He would be speaking at the 92nd Street Y a week later, his first visit to America. *His Holiness, the Dalai Lama.* I memorized the words, not even knowing if they were a name. I planned on looking them up at the library. I was excited in a way that was new. What I felt was actually quieted, a rare sense of utter well-being.

I put on my sweatshirt and sneakers to go out, for the very first time keeping something secret from Jamie. I managed to leave the apartment without our parents or her seeing me.

In the tenth row, sitting between two adult couples who probably each thought I belonged to the other, I waited for His Holiness, the Dalai Lama.

When he appeared on the stage everyone rose and applauded. He bowed and took a seat, with another man seated next to him, a translator. His Holiness bowed to his translator, looked out at the audience of thousands of people and laughed and waved.

He spoke mostly in English, pausing every few sentences to ask the translator for a particular word. I had read in the library that the Dalai Lama was the leader of Tibet, that he lived in exile in India, and that he was the fourteenth Dalai Lama, each one the living incarnation of the Buddha himself. I had asked my father who Buddha was, and he had said, "God, Allah, Jesus, Buddha—all the same."

The Dalai Lama was in New York to deliver his Five Point Peace Plan.

"The world is increasingly interdependent. I speak to you today as the leader of the Tibetan people and as a Buddhist monk devoted to the principles of a philosophy based on love and compassion."

He asked if we were willing to try compassion. He said all people want to find happiness and to avoid suffering. All people feel the same thing. He said universal compassion had great force; that once you began to feel it you could hardly stop. He laughed and seemed to want us to laugh with him. Slowly the crowd laughed with him. I looked around and laughed too.

Then he told his audience how the People's Republic of China invaded Tibet, his home, in 1949 and of his escape to India ten years later after Tibet's failed opposition. He fled across the Himalayans wrapped in blankets and carried on the back of a donkey, seventeen years-old, but already the fourteenth Dalai Lama.

At the time, I scarcely understood the Dalai Lama's words. I pictured armies crossing borders and invasions, and the image of this one man fleeing across mountains, grew clear in my imagination. My ideas were based on the castle games I played with Jamila, the limited view of a child.

Years later, when I spent time with the Dalai Lama and began to grow into an adult, I would learn from him about Chinese population transfers into Tibet, making Tibetans the second-class minority in their native land, and the state of apartheid there that forbade Tibetans their religion, their culture, their way of life, and their leader. Then I went and saw for myself. What was once Chengdu was now Sichuan; what had been Tibet was now China. I saw firsthand how a free and democratic Tibet existed only in India, in an exiled idyll, and how Tibet had grown to be a sad shell.

But that night, as a mere child, I was focused only on the man seated onstage. As he told us his story, I closed my eyes and saw his life, like a movie, in my mind. I saw a much younger Dalai Lama, a teenager who was the ruler of his land, who was unwilling to speak to the Chinese. He faced his adversaries, hoping silence and listening could be stronger than force and objection.

I saw him as a child hidden in tents and blankets, concealed in rooms like lairs, growing up being schooled and worshipped simultaneously. He played on the dirt floor of the home of his birth, sitting at meals with his devout family. He lived like any small boy, until he was found. There in Tibet, as a boy younger than my seven years, he was recognized as the reborn Dalai Lama.

"Above all, I am here as a human being who is destined to share this planet with you at this very auspicious time. We are here together as a single family."

I looked around at the many faces in the auditorium around me, not one of them was known to me. And yet it seemed it must be true—we were destined for each other. It mattered that we were sharing the planet at the same time. This revelation, the first in my life, made my throat constrict.

When his talk was over, I stood in the aisle on stiff legs. I understood the world to be larger and more meaningful than I had before and I was scared and unsure of myself. I made my way to the front. The Dalai Lama seemed to take in my whole existence in a single look. He motioned with the tilt of his head for me to come around the table, beside him. He raised his arm, and I nestled under his wing. He spoke to many people while holding me in his embrace, the crimson folds of his robe draped around me. I peered not at the holy man's face, but at the faces of the people who lined up to greet him. I thought I looked through both our eyes at the many searching eyes before us.

Most people wanted to shake his hand, to touch him. His Holiness, the Dalai Lama bowed to every person in the line, grasping each hand in his, saying over and over again the same Tibetan blessing, *Sarwa Maitri*. Many people said the words back to him. His right arm, always returning to wrap around my shoulders, was conscious of my presence there. His arm alone spoke to me, comforted me, told me to stay put, to keep attention, to patiently wait for us to talk.

In a smaller room behind the auditorium, we sat down together. There were several other monks with shaved heads, wearing robes like the Dalai Lama's, clustered nearby and speaking quietly.

The Dalai Lama spoke directly to me for the first time. "You came here alone, no parents?"

I nodded yes, suddenly scared about having left home without telling them. "I live close by."

"Why did you come today?"

"I saw your picture and it made me feel . . . like I already knew you."

"Do you know me?"

I shrugged, hoping he would say that we did know each other somehow. I thought of those man's colors, imagining the rising vapors following me into this room. "A man ran into me on the sidewalk. Then, a minute later, he got shot. He died and colors rose from his body."

His Holiness, the Dalai Lama peered at me. I let the sound of his name ripple in my ears again, *Dalai Lama, Dalai Lama, Dalai Lama.* The words soothed me.

"Maybe you saw his consciousness leaving this world. Sometimes even very young eyes are looking for enlightenment."

He touched my head. "Young one, what do you think would be the first step toward enlightenment?"

I was quiet for a long time. I didn't want to be wrong. I didn't want to disappoint the Dalai Lama.

"What you talked about today."

"I talked about a lot of things. Which?"

"Compassion."

The Dalai Lama looked pleased. "What does compassion mean?"

"It's like love. But loving with an open heart for everyone."

He signaled to one of his companions to pour us tea.

My sneakers rode the air in front of me, my legs hanging only halfway to the floor from the couch. The Dalai Lama didn't smile or touch my hair again. He leaned forward and looked at my face.

"You are looking for some explanations . . . about you, about your path."

My chin started to tremble, and I tried not to cry. I covered my face with my arm.

"You hold the answer in your own hands. It is your question to answer." Then he gently lowered my arm and smiled at me, telling me without speaking not to be frightened. "What is your name?"

That afternoon in Manhattan, the Dalai Lama saw me. He saw that I knew him, and he wondered who I was, just as I wondered who he was. He did not become my teacher that day, and not for years to come. But I found my spiritual teacher, the first step of my Dharma practice and enlightenment.

Chapter 3

Jamila

AS THE NEXT week wore on, I still didn't hear from Salam. I composed many texts and then deleted them. By Friday afternoon I was finding it hard to get a deep breath. I left work early, feeling tears pushing at my throat. His workday would end in just a couple hours. Would we miss our second weekend together without even a word about it? I could then imagine that he was gone from my life. Like that—over.

I paced my apartment and finally, my fear and desire overcame my pride and I called his cell phone. The hopeful ringing ended with his recorded message, like a punch in the stomach. I felt certain he watched his phone lighting up with my name.

In the bathroom mirror, I watched the tears roll down my face. I lost patience with myself and went to lie on the couch. I opened my journal and read what I'd written about Salam—him baking me orange currant cookies, being in the shower together, taking his penis in my mouth with the hot water washing over me. I put the journal down and went back to the bathroom.

I'd examined myself in the mirror when I was fourteen, to see if my body was changing the way David's body was changing. That day, when I discovered that puberty would betray me and separate us even further, had ended in the excruciating pain of broken bones.

This time, I noticed my eyes were bloodshot from crying. My hair was grown out from my last haircut, wavy and long. I stood up straight and checked myself out. I even lifted my shirt and looked at my small breasts and flat stomach. I looked sexy in a distraught way. I thought, *Salam's in love with me and scared.*

I dressed quickly and headed out before I could think twice.

At the bar of Salam's restaurant, I sat exposed in the modern spare room, a solitary figure. I could feel my heart pumping my blood too fast. Maybe he wasn't even there. Or at any moment he might come out of the kitchen, looking tired and under the weather but grateful to see me. He might walk up to me and bury his face in my neck, something he'd never done in front of his coworkers, and say, "I love you, I love you, I love you." Or he might walk out of the kitchen, appearing the picture of health, full of color, hair shining, with a joyous laugh and light in his eyes as he gazed at another woman he'd fallen for.

Salam passed through the curtain from the kitchen and stood in the doorway. I felt a jolt at seeing his pale angular face, the dark circles under his eyes. He looked at his watch and coughed. When he saw me, he did not smile.

"Jamila, you shouldn't have come."

The sound of his voice brought fresh pain. "I'm sorry." I felt my chin trembling. "I just wanted to see you."

"It's just that I'm not well. I'm exhausted."

"That's okay. I just wanted to see you and say hi." I couldn't look him in the face. *Just, just, just.* The rejection was overpowering.

"I'm sorry, Jamila. Give me a few days to recuperate and get back up to speed. I'll call you and we can get together to talk."

My heart seized at his choice of words. I gathered my things. We walked out to the street together.

"How are you traveling, subway or cab?" he asked. I couldn't stomach his pity. Did he imagine me riding the subway from Brooklyn to sit at his bar for fifteen minutes and then turning around to go home, rejected? It was the humiliating truth.

"I'm going to the Strand and then I'll take the train." I cringed, remembering we'd met there and maybe he would think I was making a desperate plea to remind him of our history.

"Okay, I'm in need of a cab." And with that he stuck his arm up in the air, and a taxi pulled over. I was incredulous at the speed at which this all was happening. Salam put his hand on my shoulder and kissed my cheek, as if I were his aunt.

"I'll talk to you soon, Jamila."

He was gone.

AFTER DAVID'S FIRST Buddhist retreat in England at age ten, my parents and I picked him up at JFK. He was so hyper he didn't notice that I was sad. He didn't ask about me. He talked about England. He described how the Dalai Lama told jokes and laughed all the time. David marveled at how amazing silence could be. He didn't talk for four days on his trip and suggested we try doing the same. He explained how talking prevents you from noticing your feelings and your actions, how you grow new eyes when you stop talking. I wished he'd stop talking for five minutes. That was just the car ride home.

At home, Mom unpacked David's suitcase and loaded his clothes into the washing machine. She started preparing dinner. I leaned against the kitchen counter right beside David. We stood with our hips and shoulders touching, but still he was three thousand miles away. The distance was there to stay. I understood our new separateness, as dinner was being cooked, as the washing machine churned, as my father listened to David proudly, and my mother took down plates, happy again to be four.

When we finished eating, David said, "Thanks for dinner, Mom." He stood and picked up his plate. "I'm gonna go take a shower."

We'd never taken baths or showers without being told. In fact, my mother often turned the water on for me, adjusted the temperature, and left a clean towel. I imagined David had needed to be self-sufficient while he was in England, but I was terrified that I'd fallen irreparably behind.

As David cleared his plate, my parents exchanged a look.

"Well, can't complain about that," Dad said after David left the room.

Mom looked uncertain and then with false brightness said, "Jamie, you take a bath tonight too, okay?"

My parents began clearing the table, starting with my plate.

While David showered, I folded the scarf I'd knitted for him in half and then in half again. I wrapped it in green tissue paper and tied it with brown raffia string. I took pride in the pretty square the gift made. But I felt shy about giving it.

When I heard the shower had stopped, I walked by the bathroom and saw David sitting on the toilet seat in his pajamas, one leg bent, foot up, cutting his toenails. I felt reassured that he still wore the pajamas I knew.

"I made you something." I held out the wrapped present.

David tore open the tissue paper and unfurled the plain knit purple scarf. "You made this?" He hung it around his neck and looked at the ends.

"Here, I'll show you a way to wear it." I took it back and folded it in half, put it around his neck again, and tucked the two ends through the loop, to one side. "Look in the mirror."

David went to the medicine cabinet. "I'll wear it every day."

For the first time since we'd picked him up, I felt the physical relief of being by David's side. I followed him to his room and sat on his bed while he fiddled with things on his desk, getting reacquainted with his surroundings.

He held a wooden carving of a man, the body curled up on itself like a ball. "I think the Dalai Lama wanted me to see what his students do, what they go through. So, maybe I'd do the same when I'm older."

I cleared my throat. "So, what did they do?"

David put down the carving and picked up a baseball. "Well, there's a vow you can take, to practice the Dharma. If you make that vow, then you are a bodhisattva."

"What does a bodhisattva do?"

"He takes away the suffering of others." David sat beside me.

Good, he'll become a bodhisattva and then he'll see I'm suffering.

"What are you two whispering about?" Our mother had appeared in the doorway.

"We're not whispering," we both said at once.

Mom laughed. "Still like one mind with two mouths. Jamie, I filled the tub for you. Come take your bath."

A week later, just before our tenth birthday, the two of us were sent to our uncle and aunt's house in Connecticut for a visit.

From their kitchen bay windows I could see the landscaped backyard and blue swimming pool. After breakfast, mid-week, I went up to our room to put on my bathing suit. The view from our bedroom window was of the pool as well. From every window on the backside of that house, you could see the pool. It seemed the house had been built to say, "We have a huge pool for just two people."

There was a knock on the door, and David called out, "It's me."

"Come in."

He opened the door. "You going swimming?"

"Aren't you?"

"Not right now. I want to work on the alphabet for a while."

Since he'd returned from the retreat, David had been memorizing the characters of the Tibetan alphabet, tracing them on a sketch pad, and then tenuously writing monosyllabic words.

I stood there in my one-piece bathing suit, my belly sticking out—vulnerable. There was a disproportionate sense of rejection over the fact that my brother didn't want to swim with me.

The sun was bright, and the dark green blades of grass were sharp and blunt under my bare feet. I couldn't see the roofs of the nearest houses and imagined that was the point. So different from how we lived, pressed together in the city. There were no sounds of traffic, or voices, or construction, although to my ears there was a constant drone in the unnaturally silent air. Green grass, wood fence, nothing but blue in the empty sky.

Imagining David watching me from our window upstairs, I dove into the pool and swam the full length underwater. When I surfaced on the far side, I turned and stared up at the big white house. David was not standing in the window watching me as I'd hoped. He was somewhere in the house, working on the Tibetan alphabet, copying characters, memorizing their shapes.

I saw myself from the outside, a lonely girl clinging to the side of a pool, her dark wet hair stuck to her head, in a gigantic empty back yard. There was a white glare coming off the pool, not a leaf or a bug floating on the surface, and I had a sudden and despairing awareness of the many years of childhood still to go.

The fenced-in backyard abutted some woods, and in one area they'd removed part of the fence to allow a view of the trees. A wolf appeared through that opening, delicately picking her way between the trees toward me. She paused to make sure I was alone, ears twitching in each direction. I was the only person she trusted. I raised a hand to her, and her head bobbed once in acknowledgement. I had a moment of fear. A wolf is a dangerous animal. But as she stepped into the full sun and approached the pool, I knew she was choosing me.

Inhaling a deep breath, I dove underwater. I skimmed along the bottom, back and forth like a sand snake. I did two laps without coming up. The swimming or skimming became harder. Up at the surface, the wolf bowed low, her paws neatly bent over the pool's edge, her pink tongue lapped at the cool water. I grunted as I made a wide turn, realizing I was staying down there. It was uncomfortable, it was time to come up, but I wouldn't be.

I saw myself churning underwater as David bent over his sketchpad. I felt the seismic shift that had occurred in my life. I was an immobile continent, and David was like a tectonic plate, drifting away. I had an overwhelming desire to be on my way somewhere too.

Her thirst and curiosity quenched, the wolf raised her head and licked her whiskers. Her quick ears picked up a sound from the house. A ripple ran along her muscles beneath her fur, and she turned, trotted back through the fence, and disappeared into the trees.

I was out of breath. My bathing suit snagged along the rough concrete bottom as I shut my eyes against the water.

I don't remember being hauled out of the water by my uncle, being roughly shaken, or regurgitating pool water. I was still picturing the wolf and how she ran alone in empty woods, seeking her own peace.

AFTER SALAM DISAPPEARED into a cab, I didn't go to the Strand. I rode the subway back to Brooklyn and got into bed, fully dressed, willfully ending my day. Before meeting Salam, I had made the pieces of my life into enough to sustain me. I had Grandma, and my girls at work. There were friends, and even my parents. I imagined that David was there if I needed him, and I told myself I didn't need him. Loving Salam had blown holes in all that. My life wasn't enough.

I wouldn't validate my mother's concerns, nor could I admit it to myself, but I had a twin's intuition that David was not okay. What did he really know about that part of the world? Wasn't all of Tibet under Chinese rule? He was a western Buddhist arriving from Dharamsala, the Dalai Lama's home in exile. Maybe they stopped him at the airport. He could have been detained and left to starve. I hadn't seen my brother in nearly three years.

I opened my laptop and typed in David's email address that I hadn't used in many months.

"Where are you? Call me."

That night I let my grief creep up to the edge of my bed. I could have reached out and touched that painful truth, let my fingers be bitten by it, but instead I tucked them tighter beneath my pillow.

The truth was David was too far away, in time and place for me to know how he was. I couldn't suppress my thoughts of the prescription bottle of sleeping pills in my medicine cabinet. I had not laid a hand on it in three years, but I saw it twice a day when I took down my toothbrush.

I woke up in the middle of the night and the wolf was in my room. She'd never inhabited the walls of that apartment before, but there she was with her yellow unblinking eyes glowing in the darkness. She crouched low and quiet, her large head resting on her front paws. Her soft whining filled my ears.

I crept out of bed and, without looking into the corner where the wolf lay, I half-ran to the kitchen, my chest heaving. I flipped on the light. Every dish I'd used during my week without Salam was piled high in the sink. *Why can't Salam love me?* Perhaps he couldn't love me because he sensed I was half of a whole. I heard the wolf rise in the other room. Peering through the archway between my kitchen and the dim inner rooms, I saw her bend low in a downward dog, her long snout pointing at me as she stretched languidly. I ducked out of view. From the sound of her claws on the floor, I knew she circled upon herself several times and re-settled. *I can wait,* was the message I got from her. *I can wait you out.*

I washed each plate and bowl, each fork and knife, and scrubbed the pans clean, not caring what time it was or that the dishes could stay in the sink until morning, anything to not be in my bedroom with the sleeping, biding-her-time wolf.

Chapter 4

David

MY ELATION OVER finding Lobsang and having my first encounter with him lifted my spirits and fueled my next steps. Through the newspaper man in the square, I found a translator. I felt confident that our conversation would go deep this time. I imagined that we could easily get beyond my command of Tibetan, and I wanted no barriers between us. Yonten was a village youth who had come home from Tibet University in Lhasa for the summer. I returned to Lobsang's compound the very next day, hiring a motorcycle taxi to take us. I couldn't ask Yonten to walk six miles. And now that I'd found Lobsang, I abruptly lost the need to walk that road in my single-minded search.

A westerner and a local youth getting off a motorcycle taxi in their compound was an uncommon sight. Two men, standing in the yard, watched us. I approached them and asked for Lobsang. They remained motionless and silent. Yonten spoke to them.

I had told Yonten that I was a Buddhist practitioner and had come from Dharamsala to study at Kirti Monastery. I'd said that it was very important that I speak to the young monk who had self-immolated, Lobsang, and that I needed a translator to make sure no words were lost. I was paying him twenty US dollars, a lot of money for him, and for me as well.

Yonten explained who I was and what I wanted. They spoke back to him with great emotion. I stood there as though I didn't know the language, sensing this was best. Yonten explained that I was a student at the same monastery where Lobsang had been. I pushed away my guilty feelings about how this should be true, but I had so far evaded my new teacher. The two men looked at each other and then one nodded. He turned, conveying with a jerk of his head that we could follow him.

We approached the front door of one of the ten identical houses, and the neighbor knocked. A young Tibetan woman opened the door. She looked past her neighbor at us and spoke in rapid Tibetan.

"She says Lobsang does not speak to journalists anymore, that you should go."

I nodded, having understood. "Tell her that I'm not a journalist."

Yonten did as I requested.

"Tell her that I am a student of the Dharma, a Buddhist practitioner, like Lobsang."

"I told her that already. I think I should tell her that you come from Dharamsla, from His Holiness' Namgyal Monastery. Maybe then, she lets you see Lobsang."

I spoke directly to Lobsang's caregiver in Tibetan then. "I mean him no harm. The opposite. I bring him only goodwill and wishes for health. I want to only give him blessings and briefly talk."

She stared at me a long time and then she shut the door.

"She will go ask him," Yonten said.

I nodded.

We stood there for some time. The neighbors wandered off.

It would have been people just like these neighbors who had saved Lobsang. Someone had doused the flames and rushed him to a hospital. Now he was miraculously living a fairly open life. He did not lay in hiding from the Chinese authorities, or escape to Dharamsala or elsewhere. I imagined a very limited existence, without friends or family. He was no longer a monk, but I doubted he had a job or livelihood. Yonten and I stood there a long time. He shifted impatiently on his feet.

"Mr. David, a half hour has passed. Perhaps we come another day?"

"No. Please wait a little longer. He is deciding. If I leave he will decide no forever. If I stay he will see I am serious and patient, and he will say yes."

"Yes, Mr. David."

"Just David is fine."

The door opened again.

The woman said, "You may come in and see Lobsang now." She moved aside to let us enter. She directed us to sit at a small dining table in the sparse main room, a plastic woven rug beneath our feet, there was no other furniture. I noticed a rectangular patch of clean paint on the wall and I guessed that a picture of the Dalai Lama had been taken down before we were allowed to enter. It was illegal to hang his image in your home, yet every Tibetan did. The woman exited into a second room that I hadn't guessed was there from looking at the house from the outside.

"I wonder how he affords a nurse," I said to Yonten in English.

"Nurse?"

"The caregiver, the woman."

"That is his wife."

"He's married? But he's a monk."

"He has become a layman. He abdicated his vows. Did you not know that, Mr. David?"

Lobsang emerged out of the back room and wheeled himself toward us. He parked his wheelchair next to the dining table, facing us from a few feet away.

For the first time, I was seeing Lobsang with his head uncovered. His body was bent toward his lap in a permanent twist, one ear was turned to the floor, the other to the ceiling. His ear that pointed heavenward had been transformed into a small mound of flesh with a mere hole at its top, like the mouth of a volcano. I pictured the ear was an erupting volcano. The scalding lava had geysered out and poured down his head and face, causing all this ruin, his disfigurement.

"I thought you were a journalist. Many journalists have come to see me since the self-immolation, many of them westerners too. Now I believe you are not a journalist because you look poor, and you don't have nice hiking shoes and a camera. Did you really study in Dharamsala? Who were your teachers? And what do you want from me?"

So his wife had understood what Yonten said in English, or at least picked up the words Dharamsala, Namgyal Monastery. I could see how it was a leap of faith to believe me. And Lobsang was a monk, or at least had been one. He knew that I wasn't worth my salt as a Buddhist if I wasn't devoted to my teacher.

"I've had two teachers for many years, since I was ten years old. His Holiness, the fourteenth Dalai Lama and Dilgo Khyentse Rinpoche."

Yonten, Lobsang and his wife all stared at me.

Dilgo Khyntse Rinpoche taught many monks at Kirti Monastery. He'd instructed me on the *Thirty-seven verses of the Bodhisattva* and he'd overseen my vows in Dharamsala. It was possible he'd done the same for Lobsang in Tibet.

Lobsang's one eye grew wider. "Are you studying now at Kirti?"

I continued, "I am a Buddhist practitioner, a bodhisattva, and your humble friend. I have not gone to Kirti. It's been more important to me to meet you."

Lobsang's face took on a closed, angry expression somehow, without my being able to see what exactly had changed in his stretched and taut features. His eye had flashed with interest but then grew dull again. I thought of a scorned lover, who upon hearing their lover's name felt a gleam of passion and then remembered their painful rift.

"Once I would have felt the deepest thrill to be paid a visit by an emissary of the Dalai Lama. Now, it is meaningless to me."

I pointed to the clean rectangle on the wall. "Doesn't a picture of His Holiness hang there, in your home?"

Yonten looked where I pointed and blushed deeply.

"Yes, His Holiness' picture hangs there. My wife still worships him. But the fire has taken my face and my spiritual practice."

The bedroom door opened and a tiny girl, not even a year old tottered out of the room. She held up her arms toward Lobsang and squealed loudly. He raised his bent arms forward as much as they would extend and spoke softly to her. Once again, his face moved barely a millimeter, yet I detected a new expression. I saw Lobsang's great tenderness toward the child. He lifted the girl into his lap, onto the chair with him. His wife stood in the doorway, speaking quietly to the child.

"He has fathered a child?" I said in English.

"Do you want me to ask him that, Mr. David?"

"No."

I watched father and child.

"This is my life. What I learned at Kirti cannot do anything for me now. I do not need His Holiness." Lobsang stroked his small daughter's head. "Her freedom is all I could ask for, for my wife and daughter and me to leave here."

Lobsang rolled his wheelchair into the back bedroom and shut the door behind him.

Yonten and I took another motorcycle taxi back to the square, where I paid him and we shook hands and walked in opposite directions. As I walked the dirt road toward my guest house, I worried for the hundredth time in the past few weeks if I should have been going to Kirti Monastery. Perhaps I was ready to start my studies. I might call His Holiness too, I thought, to share with him how I'd met Lobsang.

From a distance, I saw a white piece of paper tacked to the private front door of my guest house.

I gently removed the folded paper with a shaking hand. In my four weeks in Sichuan, there had been no messages for me. It was written by my landlord in Tibetan, which I could still barely read. There were only two words I understood, *Kirti Monastery*.

Instead of entering my room, I walked directly back to the square. I would translate the note at the Internet café I had never entered before.

The note was from Gayto Rinpoche, my new teacher at Kirti.

> *I am concerned that you have not shown up for your appointment to begin your studies with me. I have called your cellular phone numerous times and written you few emails. Because you have not arrived at Kirti Monastery and I am aware that you have arrived in Tibet, I have contacted your emergency contact in New York, Margot Erev, mother.*

I vaguely remembered writing to the monastery from Dharamsala, after the Dalai Lama had recommended me to them. I'd sent Gayto Rinpoche my flight information, the name of my guest house, my phone number, and email and my emergency contact.

There was another email that made me feel the severity of my recent behavior even more.

Jamie had written me two short lines. *Where are you? Call me.*

Walking back to my guest house, I looked around me at the dirt-packed road, the tuberosa and yarrow in bloom, the shredded clouds in a clear blue sky. The surrounding hills on the eastern edge of the Tibetan plateau were the bright and forest greens of a Himalayan summer. It was very hot, and I felt the unnecessary heft of my long-sleeved shirt as though I had just arrived in this place that day, as though I hadn't seen it yet. The passage of time had been an unnoticed detail. My only devotion had been to Lobsang.

In my room, I unburied my cell phone from the bottom of my suitcase, plugged it into the one outlet by my bed, and watched it come to life.

Tethered to the wall by the charger cord, I called Jamila. It seemed nothing short of a miracle that she answered. Suddenly there was my twin sister's voice in my ear.

"David! I can't believe it's you."

"You asked me to call. I'm calling."

"Where are you? You're not at the monastery?"

"How do you know that?"

"They're looking for you. They contacted Mom. You missed our birthday."

"I haven't met them yet. I've been taking a break, seeing Tibet." I couldn't tell Jamila how I'd been spending my time pursuing Lobsang.

"What have you seen?"

"What?"

"You said you've been seeing Tibet."

"Oh, I've just been walking a lot."

Jamila sighed. It was a sound I imagined her making when alone. I tried to picture her on the other side of the planet, but I didn't know if she was home or at work, and either way I couldn't put walls or furniture or any of her belongings around her. I didn't know her world anymore.

"Jamie, where are you right now?"

"What do you mean?"

"I'm trying to picture you. Are you at work? At home? It sounds weird there . . . I hear beeping."

"I'm fine now. But I'm in Bellevue Hospital. I had an episode."

Rising to my feet, I jerked the phone from the charger and kicked a plastic garbage can across the room where it bounced off the wall.

"David? Did you just throw something?"

"Dammit, Jamie! What happened?" Like a tidal wave, the profound loneliness and rejection I'd been feeling since arriving in Tibet crashed over me. Use everything, I tried to remind myself, this too is the path.

Jamie didn't respond.

I took a deep breath and righted the garbage can, pretending it was a sacred object. "I'm sorry. I'm not ready for this."

"Neither was I," she whispered.

"I'm sorry, Jamie. It's been really bad here. Tell me what happened."

"I took pills. What's been really bad there?"

Jamie's episodes had never seemed purely attention-seeking, but didn't feel like true suicide attempts either. I had no idea how to gage this one. What pills did she have and could they have been deadly? And if so, why hadn't they been?

"Don't worry about it. It's you I'm concerned about. I'm sorry I'm being such a jerk." Our lives were like a tug of war game. There was a length of rope that couldn't be stretched. If I tried to grow or move further afield, she was yanked, and always yanked back. We were tethered together, even when we didn't know it. "Why did you do it?"

"I don't know." Jamie sighed, this time with genuine fatigue. "I'm in love with someone."

"You're in love? That doesn't explain it. The opposite."

She was silent, and I was afraid the call had been dropped. "Jamie?"

"It just hurts too much—even the happiness."

It was on this call that I first heard the name Salam. In those two syllables, I discerned my sister's joy and her downfall. I felt the heights she had been traversing and her trip back down.

"Are they releasing you?"

"Yes. Tomorrow."

"Alone?"

Jamie actually laughed. "We're thirty now. Yeah, alone."

"I'll book a flight. I'll be there in a few days."

The following day, two hours before my flight to Lhasa, a boy ran past my guest house shouting in Tibetan, words I didn't recognize. The sounds of doors slamming and people running immediately followed. Other voices shouted the same words the boy had, some sort of warning. I ran into the street, where dozens of people of all ages rushed past me. Their urgency infected me. I reached for the arms of people running by, trying to stop them.

"What's happening? Please, do you speak English? Anyone!"

No one stopped, no one spoke my language, and no one wanted to slow down to speak to the westerner who had appeared in their village from nowhere.

Inside my guest room, my bags were all packed. After that day, I'd never see those four walls again, nor all of Sichuan perhaps. I pulled my door shut tightly, and without locking it, I ran with all the villagers toward whatever it was they ran toward or away from.

In the square where I'd first seen Lobsang at the newspaper stand, the villagers pooled into a crowd. People craned their necks to see what was happening, but there was nothing to see. One or two stall keepers stood beside their stalls expectantly. The air was still and electrified. The same unknown and ominous sounding words moved through the crowd like a stuttered prayer, broken and lacking the synchronicity of chanting. *No, not like a chant*, I thought, it sounded like a curse, passed from mouth to mouth.

A collective scream erupted from the crowd of villagers. I was shoved as the crowd tried to back up from the square's center.

Young and strong, like a marathon runner, a man ignited in flames appeared from one corner and sprinted diagonally across the square. He was not a monk. His all black clothing was on fire from shoulders to pant cuffs. Flames leapt from his body, licked at his face and thick black hair and reached to surround his hands.

The young man's face was not yet damaged and his expression was awed, quietly excited and determined, probably in shock and coursing with adrenaline. His gracefulness and strength existed in opposition to the blazing blanket of death he wore.

A scream tore from my throat. Policemen, the Chinese Authorities, burst through the screaming crowd, pistols raised. I don't know how many of them fired, how many times each one might have shot him, but his gait abruptly altered. His legs seemed to still have the command to run, but his chest had stopped in place. The bullets, momentarily acting as straight pins, tacked him to the air. He stood upright for several seconds, his body in a spasm of flux between his fiery sprint and a chest full of bullets. He fell.

I knew, and the whole crowd knew, he was dead. I couldn't take my eyes off his fallen body. And then I saw what I didn't realize I was waiting for. A thin palette of Himalayan hues, poppy red and the yellow of turmeric, rose off him like a wisp of steam from a cup of barley tea, a split second of light and color.

"Cover him," I shouted to no one. I imagined my sister was beside me, as she had been the other time I saw a young man shot. But this time, Jamila was thousands of miles away, perhaps in her own fiery hell, completely ignorant to what I'd just seen, not knowing that men were lighting themselves on fire in growing numbers in the name of Tibet.

With their guns now raised at the crowd, the police barked orders. People backed away quickly. The police could open fire on the crowd if they wanted to. The world wasn't watching. I heard weeping all around me. A child I played soccer with was standing nearby, shaking violently. He threw himself against the man beside him and bawled loudly. His father, I presume, lifted him, even though he was as old as eight, and the boy wrapped his legs around his dad as they turned away from the square.

"Cover him." I wept with no father to take me in his arms.

The policemen forcibly emptied the square of on-lookers, shouting and poking with their batons. No one raised their voice or challenged the police. No one stayed with the body of the self-immolator. We were all afraid of the guns.

Chapter 5

Jamila

MY COPY OF *Sweets of Panjab* with the inscription that read "Please" lay open on Salam's kitchen table to the persimmon croquettes recipe. We had smudged the page with butter and caramelized persimmon. If Salam hadn't become my lover, those pages would have remained pristine, the book's spine unbroken.

Salam's phone rang. He answered it in the kitchen with a bright American "Hello," before his Indian accent transformed into a bubbling brook of Hindi. He walked out of the room without looking my way. Without understanding his words, I imagined I heard their intimacy. I stayed in the kitchen and tried to concentrate on the recipe. I read and re-read the next step, *chip in small pieces of cold butter,* but my hands were all thumbs. His voice in the other room, so smooth, reminded me of my nickname for him, Silky.

It had been my idea that we bake one of his recipes; I'd brought his book and all the ingredients, as though for the first time we needed an activity. We'd begun baking as soon as I arrived, the new undeniable bridge slung between us. I wanted to make love and talk, in that order, but we baked.

I stayed in the kitchen, almost holding my breath, trying to give him privacy for the call. I stared at the glossy cover of his book, remembering him holding it in one hand while he spoke at the bookstore, and how he looked at me while he signed it. He had looked afraid.

I wasn't being totally honest with Salam. I hadn't divulged my true feelings. I also hadn't told him important things about my past. I started to share stories about David's discovery of

Buddhism as a child, how the Dalai Lama became his teacher and mentor, and his trips to India to study under revered lamas, but I left out my response to these changes. Salam didn't know about my long history of self-harm or years of therapy. Yet still, when we discussed David, he'd astutely commented, "That must have been hard for you, the other twin." Salam had showed more interest in me than in the miracle of David's life, and he intuited that David's spiritual pursuits had left me lonely.

I'd imagined telling Salam about the two occasions on which I'd seriously hurt myself. I sometimes felt the words crouching behind my lips. But I was afraid he would pity me or be disgusted. I would be too ugly, too foreign.

Salam stepped back into the kitchen and picked up a piece of persimmon, coated in sugar, lemon, and corn starch. He chewed the raw fruit and sucked his fingers.

Salam layered the fruit mixture and pastry in a baking pan, forgetting to include me in the process. He slid the pan into the hot oven.

His eyes on the empty bowl between us, he said, "This is my wife's recipe. Jamila, I'm married."

I gasped. A small blade entered my stomach. For the first time since I'd met Salam, I had a hard, ugly feeling toward him. I recalled sitting at his bar, eating this same dessert, and hoping he'd be happy to see I'd tracked him down. I had told him it was my favorite, after we ate one of each.

"You've taken the credit," I said, though that didn't begin to convey what I was objecting to.

"The recipe? It doesn't matter. They all come from somewhere."

"I think it matters. Because you're cheating on your wife and you've been lying to me!"

Salam made a hurt guttural sound. He dropped his head against mine. His hair smelled of primrose and sandalwood. I wanted to sink my fingers into its mink. I wanted to pull him close and to push him away.

"Please, Jamila, I can't expect you to understand, but there are extenuating circumstances."

"Like what?"

"She knows about us."

"You told her you're having an affair?"

"Sort of. We had an arranged marriage three years ago. She's from a modern Hindu family, like me, but our families introduced us, made our match. Her name is Chitra. She's a good wife. We've been through some hard times from the start, but she agreed I could come to America for this apprenticeship, for a year without her."

"Unless India is another planet with a whole other set of rules, I don't understand! Do you have an open marriage?" I pressed my hands to my thighs because they wanted to slap his face.

He grimaced. "We didn't plan for this. But other things have gone downhill. It's changed."

The oven timer beeped. Salam pulled the pan from the oven automatically. His desserts did not burn, even while he talked of his infidelity.

We stood over the cooling pan, wordlessly, as never before. My first urge was to leave and get home where I could be alone. But when I pictured entering my apartment, I saw the wolf, leaping to her feet at my early return. My heart raced while my body didn't move an inch.

We ate the dessert with our fingers, right out of the baking pan. I felt like crying while I tasted the burnt sugar and fruit. I still wanted to leave, but I desperately wanted to just make love as though I didn't know anything he'd told me. Salam brushed crumbs off the corner of my mouth. He placed his hand on the back of my neck, working his way under my hair. Pressing the bones at the back of my skull with his forefinger and thumb, he pulled my mouth onto his. I tasted his warm pastry-sweet tongue. With my eyes closed, I allowed myself the beautiful free-falling that making love with Salam brought over me. I kissed him back, my hands reaching underneath his shirt.

After we made love, he leaned against the headboard, still naked under the sheets.

"I know this hardly makes sense," he said, "but there's a reason why Chitra is okay with it. She's not happy about it, but she's given her permission."

I was stretched out beside him, also naked. *This was the last time*, I thought to myself.

"That was her on the phone, obviously. She's arriving tomorrow, Jamie."

I wrapped my arms around myself. There were three of us in the bed, but only I seemed to notice. I had been sleeping with a near stranger who had just told me he already belonged to someone else. Salam and I were not a *we*. I had been mistaken.

I was on a precipice, high above solid ground, reminiscent of the park roof I had actually leapt from, hoping to break something.

WHEN DAVID RETURNED from India the summer we were fourteen, he had physically changed. Seeing him in running shorts the day after he returned, I knew our bodies were no longer alike. Previously, the same light blond hair had covered our bean-pole legs. I was embarrassed to observe the thick, dark hair he had grown.

"Do you want to go running around the reservoir?" David had asked, an invitation that was clearly an afterthought.

"I don't run. Actually, you don't either."

"I got a lot of exercise in Dharamsala. We hiked up this huge hill every day to get from our guest house to the monastery." With a distant smile, he added, "Longo and I often ran all the way back down."

After David left, I stripped and stood on the toilet seat to see my body in the medicine cabinet mirror. I thought I hadn't grown at all that summer. But in my reflection in the mirror there was the beginning of a waist and a slight flair where previously my hips had been perfectly straight lines. I already had a small patch of pubic hair and small high breasts that had required a bra since the seventh grade. I stepped down and moved up close to the mirror to stare into my eyes.

Our faces were not twin faces anymore.

Our eyes were still the same transparent blue, but told different stories. Mine looked insecure and lost. Why had David's eyes conveyed so much peace, so much control?

I wanted to run away and not turn back. Thinking of myself at the bottom of my uncle's swimming pool, I felt the need for escape all over again, for my own life to take me somewhere. I wanted a self-inflicted solitude, instead of being left alone by David.

In the mirror, I saw the wolf's face looking back at me. Her yellow eyes were full of knowing, acute instincts. But I never used the wolf to positive ends. She could possess me, but I could never master her. Her ears flicked, picking up on danger nearby. She licked her whiskers and showed her teeth again.

I stalked down West End Avenue alone, carrying no backpack, no possessions. In the playground, a lone mother pushed her child on the swing. A park custodian in a green jumpsuit dragged a garbage can on wheels, sweeping litter into a dustpan on a pole. I approached the park building where he kept his can, broom, and dustpan.

The building was one story high, painted tan, with dark green trim. A narrow concrete walkway surrounded the building, and beyond the concrete lay a tiny stretch of green grass. A six-foot-tall chain-link fence divided the concrete from the grass.

I dug the toes of my high-top sneakers into the diamond links of the fence and climbed to the top in three quick moves, flung one leg over the top rail, and straddled the fence. If I stood upright, I could reach the roof of the building. After making a fast upright lunge, I stood atop the fence's top rail and placed both hands on the warm roof of the building.

I pulled myself up onto the roof. Brushing the gravel from my palms, I crossed to the front side of the building, where I could look down on the playground.

Across the yard, the park custodian spotted me.

"Hey, get down from there!"

I shook my head back and forth, like a wolf shaking off fresh raindrops. With a quick look at the concrete below, I closed my eyes and took one step forward.

The impact and the excruciating pain radiating up my arm forced my eyes open. I was not a free and wild animal. I was a girl alone in a park, staring up at the sky, having done something very wrong. I cried like a young child then, full of overwhelming grief. The park custodian called for an ambulance. I rode to the same hospital we had been born in. But this time I was there alone.

After my family arrived, the emergency-room doctor wrapped my broken arm in a cast from my wrist to armpit. The doctor assumed it was an accidental fall, and my parents went along with this. Maybe they truly believed it was an accident. Or maybe we all allowed for this deceit because I was already seeing my therapist Anne and had been making good progress. We seemed to be in unspoken agreement that I was going to have to struggle.

For the six weeks that my arm was in a cast, David was the one who washed my hair. My mother would promise to do this for me but she inevitably had three other things to do before she could begin.

My father asked, "Why do you need to wash your hair, it's only six weeks?"

I sat on the edge of the tub while David stood and massaged my head to a thick lather, then I knelt and tilted my head over the tub as he poured bowl after bowl of water over my hair. I pressed a washcloth to my eyes with my good hand. David hummed while he worked. I loved and hated him for the same reasons.

THE NIGHT SALAM told me he was married, I tried to sleep over anyway, staying where I was safe from myself. Leaving him and returning home presented worse danger. But like a forest animal who hunts at night, I felt the planet's rotation toward dawn, and I couldn't stay with Salam to see the sun come up.

I dressed in the dark, but woke Salam up when was I ready to leave. I shook him awake.

He'd given me a set of keys to his apartment, two plain keys on a silver key ring; I held these out to him in the darkness.

He sat up in bed. "What's this?"

"I'm going. I won't need these anymore."

I fled, wishing Salam could stop me, but knowing he couldn't or wouldn't. I reached my apartment in Brooklyn just as the first rays of sun cracked open the sky. As I unlocked and opened my front door, I heard growling before I saw the wolf. In the corner of the kitchen, her bared teeth glowed. Her muzzle and silvery face emerged out of the shadows. Her fur was raised along her spine. She stared at me with yellow eyes, alert and focused. Her black lips curled back over her fangs with her panting. The air was dank from her breath.

I squeezed shut my eyes and thought of drinking espresso from Salam's kitchen machine, or walking through Soho crying tears of laughter, giddy with our infatuation, feeling my crush even on the clothes he wore. I remembered him measuring my stomach with his hands. And how he'd pressed his lips on my ear saying, "I'm loving you," somehow meaning less than I love you.

Yet more than wanting to be with Salam, or to hear from David and know that he was okay, I longed to remake myself as the wolf. Sheer will would take me to her world, a world without language, without convention. Instinct, the same mapping that told every animal the behaviors of its forebears, would guide my life. I would hunt. I would know the scent of man, of fire, of horse, of rain. I would sleep in snatches. I could run or sleep all day when it was called for. The wolf was built for extremes. A slave to my instincts, I'd actually be free.

I began circling my apartment. Like an animal that had never been indoors, I stalked the perimeter warily. The rhythm of my gait eventually drummed a directive into my head.

I went to the bathroom and opened the medicine cabinet. I'd ignored the bottle of sleeping pills, my old roommate's prescription, for the past three years. But I'd never forgotten it. I dumped the contents of the bottle into my cupped hand. On the closed lid of the toilet seat, I counted out the tablets by twos. There were thirty-six. I left them sitting there on the toilet and fled the bathroom. Maybe I could escape.

I followed a blind path through the apartment again, the side of my head, my shoulder and my hip skimming the walls. I pushed furniture aside that blocked my passage, until the circuit led me back to the bathroom. My own panting turned into a whine.

My hands were paws upon the floor. My lips and tongue, picking up the tablets, formed a black muzzle turned sideways against the toilet lid to lap up the pills, like so many pieces of food. Crouching on the floor on all fours, I licked the pills off the toilet two by two, swallowing hard. I took sips of water when I could no longer swallow. Eighteen mouthfuls, thirty-six pills. Take me, I thought, I'm you.

AWAKENED BY THE doorbell, I leaned against the intercom in my kitchen, pressing the button to allow someone into my building. I fell asleep again, standing upright, leaning on the door. Loud pounding woke me. I tugged open the door to find a young Indian woman glaring at me. She wore jeans with a buttoned-up shirt. Her black hair was very long, hanging loose over each breast. I had no idea who she was.

"Can I help you?" My speech was slurred.

And right before she answered, I knew.

"I'm Chitra. I've come to tell you Salam is very sick. You'd be wise to stay away from him." She had a heavy Indian accent. Her eyes took in the full length of me, and it seemed she registered something amiss, then she turned to leave.

"Wait," I cried. My tongue was thick and my vision darkened. She turned back and her expression grew alarmed.

I collapsed to the floor like a puppet with cut strings.

What must have been hours later my eyes opened painfully. Inches in front of me was a pool of pinkish vomit with the partially-digested tablets. My mouth was dry and my head throbbing. I groaned and rolled away from my own mess.

He's married. Chitra was here.

My stomach heaved. I dry-retched over and over. When my stomach convulsions finally stopped, I cried like a kid, wishing someone would hear me. I bawled and discovered that I was glad to be bawling, glad to be alive.

I scraped myself off the floor and went to the phone. My mind was clear. I called 911.

"I need an ambulance. For me. I've taken pills, an overdose."

During every waking hour I spent in Bellevue's psychiatric ward, I tried to imagine what happened in my apartment between me swallowing thirty-six sleeping pills and Salam's wife appearing at my door. I filled in my story where there was none, creating a Chitra based on the scraps of information Salam had given and what I could remember of our encounter. Telling myself a story, even this one, was comforting. I conjured in my mind a heroine who felt toward me both disdain and empathy in equal measure.

My imagined Chitra crouched down beside me and touched my chest to see if I was breathing, "Get up. What's the matter with you?" She pressed two delicate fingers against my wrist, checking my pulse, and sat back to contemplate my lifeless face.

"*Pee-uh.*" She uttered the Hindi word for *shit*, which Salam had taught me.

Then Chitra had inhaled, bent over me, and blew air into my mouth. Wiping her mouth on her sleeve, she watched.

Nothing.

Chitra placed one hand on my forehead, tilted my head back, and gave me mouth-to-mouth. After five forced breaths, I gagged. She roughly rolled me on my side, and I threw up on my kitchen floor.

Chitra's knees touched my back. She asked, "Did you take pills?"

I confessed to the imagined version of my lover's wife. Perhaps I really did.

This part I do remember. Chitra stood over me, staring down at my inert body. Even in that half-asleep moment, I realized what poor competition I was.

She repeated, "Salam is ill," and after a pause, "I'm going now."

Chitra, whose life I'd been stealing from, had possibly saved mine.

My cellphone on the hospital nightstand rang. I glanced at the screen and was in total shock to see "David" on the screen. Before snatching up the phone, I looked to the open door, hoping no one would enter.

Chapter 6

David

IN THE BEIJING Airport at three o'clock in the morning, I walked along the disinfected, gleaming corridors between terminals with everything I owned in my army-navy backpack hulking behind me. I was the only person who had been in the square the night before who was now here, at an international airport, escaping. The short distance from the Sichuan square where the scent of burning flesh had filled my nose just ten hours earlier, felt greater than the seven thousand miles I would fly to New York. Every other person, even the Chinese authorities who shot and killed the new self-immolator, were stuck there.

I pictured Lobsang appearing in the airport corridor, his ear bent to the ground, his wooden wheelchair pivoting to face me. But his presence here was an impossibility.

Maybe I was just like a journalist, a witness who could leave at any time.

I tried to re-focus my thoughts. Yes, I was leaving Lobsang, who was like a clipped bird, forever tethered to the land which took his wings. I was leaving the dead man in the square, who was every Tibetan in occupied Tibet who would choose death over being torn away from their way of life, their culture, and their holy leader. But I was going to Jamila. By looking more to who I was returning to, and less at who I was leaving, I was able to hold my dissected parts together. Focusing on Jamila allowed me to continue standing and walking on my two feet, allowed me to find my gate and settle my pack on the floor, outwardly calm as I waited for my flight. Going to Jamila was a giving act; she needed me. I could do something for her, and that was more than I could say for my presence in the square that very day, a mere witness, or my month in Tibet, an interloper.

If one does not conquer one's own hatred, one will continually fight external enemies. The more one fights them, the more such enemies will multiply. Therefore, with the armies of loving-kindness and compassion, to tame one's own mind is the practice of the bodhisattva.

While my plane sat on the runway waiting for take-off, I hoped the rising wave of my vow would carry me. The Chinese occupation of Tibet had caused Lobsang to set himself on fire. A man in New York had caused my sister to swallow a bottle of sleeping pills. Were they my enemies? Did Lobsang and now this second self-immolator multiply their own enemies by fighting them the only way they knew how? Did Jamie?

In my native land, waves of attachment to friends and kin surge, hatred for enemies rages like fire. To abandon my native land is the practice of a bodhisattva.

It had been three years since I'd seen my sister. Those waves of attachment to her, and my parents and grandmother, and even the city of my childhood would crash over me in less than a day, when I stepped off that airplane. Jamie herself was my native land, and though I didn't want to abandon her, I didn't know how to live in that land either.

I walked out of JFK airport in Queens as the dawn turned the sky from gray to pink. I stepped onto the airtrain which would bring me to the subway and a train to Brooklyn to Jamie's apartment. The day emerged, skimpy trees and buildings blurred past, cars and semi-trucks on the Expressway snaked in two directions, soundless through the sealed windows. The colors of Tibet were leeched away, replaced by gray. I had a sudden, urgent need for His Holiness. I wanted to be enveloped in his burgundy robe, safe in his embrace. I was longing for comfort, when what I should have been asking myself was how I could ease Jamie's pain. But the world I had just left continued to feel more real than the world I'd just entered.

As the subway approached my transfer at Jamaica Station, the scenery grew even more condensed, uglier. My heart rate accelerated in opposition to the train's reduced speed. I exited and crossed through a heavy intersection to get to my train. Livery cars and yellow cabs weaved around me. Pedestrians crammed together at each corner. Drivers honked their horns as they closely skirted each other and the pedestrians. I closed my eyes and at once recognized the smells of exhaust and fast food and garbage that were omnipresent.

With the sun fully risen, it was already warm and my clothes, boots, and hulking backpack were all too heavy for the city. Dozens of pedestrians rushed past, looking through me. I felt an instinct for avoidance, yet there was a part of me that wanted to be where the action was. I felt the tug of two Davids. I was a boy from the city who could feed off the excitement that reared its head all around me. Yet I was also the other David, who resisted the flood of heightened emotion and ego.

Though the bodhisattva sees that in all phenomena there is no coming and going, He strives solely for the sake of beings.

I let the vow flow with my breath and pulse, hoping to calm myself. I tried to feel the Dalai Lama's cupped hands encircling my head, bestowing a blessing.

I was repeating my vows, the root text, the thirty-seven verses on the practice of the bodhisattva, first sworn when I was fourteen. It strummed through me with my heartbeat. I heard the voice of my old teacher, Khyenste Dilgo Rinpoche, too: "I don't know when these vows will serve you, but they will."

I entered the dark cave of Jamaica Station, looking for the subway that would take me to Jamie's apartment in Brooklyn.

I must have been lost in thought, staring blindly. I thought I was imagining a Tibetan face before me when suddenly my vision focused, and I saw I was sitting directly across from a smiling Tibetan woman. Her straight brown hair was parted in the middle and tied back in a ponytail, her almond eyes twinkled at me, her face had the perfectly symmetrical qualities I'd grown so used to in Sichuan, a face that seemed carved by water and wind. While I stared in confusion, she continued to smile and nodded a greeting at me. *Namaste.* I had to look around to see if I was already in New York or still in Tibet. We were already hurtling underground through the East River, along an artery into the great body of the city.

"You're from Tibet?" I whispered, my voice having gone dry from disuse.

She laughed. "I was on your flight from Beijing. I had a feeling you were coming from Tibet too."

I cleared my throat. "You were in Tibet?"

"Yes, I went to see my children. My grown-up children. Here, I'm a nanny. My new babies."

"You can travel freely?" I knew from my time in Dharamsala that most Tibetans who left did so secretly, through the mountains on foot, and could never return.

She tapped her purse with a conspiratorial smile. "US Passport. I'm an American citizen too." Her smile was contagious.

"I bet it was nice to see your children." I smiled back.

"Ah. My joy. My daughter will make me a grandma soon. I'm Pema." She leaned forward and held out her hand.

"I'm David." I realized that speaking to Pema was the most I'd spoken to any Tibetan while I was there, except Lobsang and Yonten. It saddened me knowing they were becoming a memory with every mile I travelled. "Your name means Lotus."

Tibetans stuck to a few dozen names, it seemed. I constantly met Tibetans who bore the same names, and they each had auspicious meanings: Lobsang—noble minded, Jampa—loving kindness, Tenzin—holder of the teachings, Yonten—good qualities.

She laughed. "You know some Tibetan!"

Pema looked at me warmly, making me think of the well-worn tenet of seeing a fellow human as your mother in another lifetime.

"Did you find what you were looking for in Tibet, David?"

Pema and I looked each other in the eye. She wanted nothing more than to know if a stranger found what he was looking for. I wanted nothing more than to answer her truthfully.

"I didn't do what I went there to do. And I didn't mean to leave so soon. A lot went wrong."

Pema's smile changed, becoming knowing and sad at the same time. "That sounds like Tibet. I hope you find your peace, David. This is me!" Pema stood to get off the subway, her smile turning a hundred watts again. *"Sarwa Maitri!"*

"Sarwa Maitri," I called to the closing doors. Loving Kindness.

I'd noticed the thin silver wedding ring on Pema's hand. I imagined her in Lhasa seated outdoors at a table covered in food, laughing with her grown children and her long-distance husband, her family who she saw every few years at best. I imagined the bedroom she was given in a brownstone in Brooklyn, where she lived with the children who she called "her babies," who loved her rambunctiously. I imagined the young Tibetan man, her future-husband, who many years ago bought her that thin silver ring, in love with her smile.

Since leaving Tibet, I'd lived through several days already and I felt like I'd travelled across worlds and centuries both. I wanted nothing more than to arrive at Jamie's door and get inside and away from the people and streets of New York.

After what must have been thousands of steps in this direction, with the thread of twins pulling us toward each other for the past three days, it was with disbelief that I saw Jamie slumped on her stoop, leaning against the side-railing, her long hair hiding her face. Her bare arms looked pale and thin. She appeared to be asleep. Before I could call out to her, she opened her eyes.

Jamie stumbled to her feet and rushed to me.

She was only a few inches shorter than me, same long limbs, same brown wavy hair—my twin. Held in my sister's embrace, I took up the vow's refrain again.

*Now that I have this great ship, a precious human life, so hard
to obtain, I must carry myself and others across the ocean of samsara.*

I let the vow flow with my breath, a vow and an aspiration.

"Are you okay?"

She nodded and pulled back to look at me. "You're so skinny,
and tan. And what's going on with your hair?"

I rubbed my hand over my head. "I don't know. Last time I
checked it was shaved."

"It's not anymore."

"It's been quite a journey."

I followed Jamie upstairs to her apartment. We went into
the living room and fell on the couch, our legs shooting out in
front of us identically. She reached behind me to turn on a lamp.
Tacked on the wall was a photo of Jamie with a young black girl,
both of them touching the girl's big belly—one of her pregnant
teens.

"I don't know what I'd do right now if you weren't here."
Jamie's eyes flicked across the room, looking like they distrusted
the space. She searched my face for answers to all of it, and I was
afraid she found none.

"How are you doing?" I already knew not to tell her what was
visible at a glance. She looked wrecked, with dark rings around
her eyes.

"I only just got home. I haven't really slept in three days."
She plucked at the loose threads of a hole in her jeans. "I'm not
even sure who broke up with who."

"You and Salam? So, it's over?"

"I think so. We haven't spoken in days. He doesn't know about
any of this." She gestured vaguely, as though the walls around us
were the issue. "Nothing lasts. Right?"

"And everything ends," I said too lightly.

Jamie narrowed her eyes at me, critically. "Thanks, David, for
trying, but do I really need a lesson on impermanence from you?"

I cringed.

"I'm sorry. Would you be my brother? Lasting, not ending?"

"I will."

"What time is it?" Jamie suddenly looked drained of all energy.

I looked at my watch. "It's almost eight."

"Is eight too early to go to bed?"

"Not if you've been up for three days."

We made up the couch for me to sleep on. Before Jamie went to bed I asked her if she had plans for the next day, the weekend.

"Not really."

I knew she was holding out, hoping that Salam would call her.

"We could go to Coney Island?" I offered.

"If the batting cages are open, I could swing a bat." She tried to smile. "Goodnight, David."

Alone in her living room, I turned on CNN and muted the TV. The endless roll of news coverage was of an industrial fire in Texas, a rescue of forty miners in South America, a bombed marketplace in Iraq. And then the screen filled with a vivid image of the streets of Lhasa. I sat up, clutching the remote, but afraid to bring back the sound. A mob of monks in red robes pushed up against a line of plastic police shields, a massive physical confrontation. Monks in the capital were rising up against the Chinese occupation. A thousand monks were arrested. If I was still in Sichuan, I wouldn't know this was happening— so nearby in Lhasa. News of protests was thoroughly suppressed inside the country.

Then the screen was filled with a grainy black and white photo, a close-up of one man. I'd never seen Lobsang's face before the fire had melted and stretched his features, but I knew him immediately. A younger, handsome monk stared at the camera. My chest tightened at the sight of him. Across the bottom of the screen it read, "Wave of self-immolations set off in Tibet in protest of the Chinese suppression of Tibetan way of life. First monk to turn self-immolator, known only as Lobsang, appears to have started current wave amongst monks and civilians alike.

Believed to have survived but whereabouts unknown. Chinese government declares self-immolation illegal."

I felt soft and exposed like a turtle without his shell. My legs shook uncontrollably as I stared at the screen. At that very moment in Lhasa, Tibetan monks were throwing rocks through police car windows and into the mob of Chinese police behind their plastic shields. Buddhist monks practicing violent protest. It was incomprehensible to me and added to the surreal feeling I had being in New York City, my whereabouts unknown to everyone except Jamie.

MY JOURNEY INTO Tibet began sixteen years earlier with my first visit to Dharamsala. The Dalai Lama's home in exile lay directly across the Himalayan Mountains in India. It was often referred to as *Tibet in exile*, a safe haven where Tibetan Buddhism was the way of life, practiced freely, upheld and revered.

For the past three years, I had been safe and secure in Dharamsala, able to foster my Buddhist practice within the realm of His Holiness, the fourteenth Dalai Lama. But then I was thrown into a reverse exile, when my esteemed teacher and friend since I was eight years-old, decided I had learned all I could under his tutelage and sent me to the Kirti Monastery, to Tibet, a land he could not enter.

On that first trip to Dharamsala when I was fourteen, the bus ride from Delhi to Dharamsala took ten hours. I listened to John Lennon through my Discman headphones, as the bus made a thousand lurching turns and no stops. If I was fourteen, then Longo was twenty-four. Our encounter a few hours earlier at the Delhi airport baggage claim had been the first time I'd seen him since England. I had recognized him right away, but his eyes had passed right over me. A young monk gathered the arriving students together and led us to our bus.

In the villages where we slowed to pass through, there mingled monks in red robes, Tibetans in traditional red and yellow clothing, and modern Indians in Western slacks and dress shirts. There were also backpackers and hippies from around the world. Everyone walking the dusty roads, moving in both directions, like leaf-cutter ants each with their green scrap of leaf—their bright burdens, all supporting the same heart center, their queen.

Beneath our bus's wheels the road dropped away, as we wound higher and higher into the Himalayas. Mist like an animate being—lunged and dragged itself around the bus and the livery sedans, hung with tassels and deities inside their windshields. The mist engulfed people riding on scooters, travelers on foot, and swallowed whole cows. It crept along the roads, scaling the mountain and reaching for the sun.

The closer we drew to Dharamsala, the greener the mountains became. I put away my Discman and leaned forward on the back of the seat in front of me, taking in the place we were entering. Longo too seemed riveted by the looming land, the otherworldliness of it all. In ten hours, I'd observed him repeatedly but never saw him looking at me.

The town of Dharamsala had shaped itself around His Holiness's palace and the Namgyal Monastery, three miles higher up in McLeod Ganj. As our bus wound through the muddy streets of Dharamsala, we joined with other crawling buses, taxis, bicyclists, tethered donkeys, and free cows. Our bus lumbered along the curvy narrow streets. When Longo slid open his window, I did the same.

I leaned out, inhaling the incense air. The Dalai Lama's significance grew larger for me. This was a city built around him, because he'd come. Tibetan prayer flags and pictures of His Holiness—photos, posters, tapestries of his face in various poses adorned the walls and windows of most shops. I was shocked to see a tearful Western woman in bell bottoms and a lacy blouse tightly embracing a young monk in robes. Another monk pulled a pack of cigarettes from his robe, offered one to the monk standing next to him and lit up.

The sidewalk cafés served tourists from around the world—white young men with dreadlocks, Scandinavian blondes wearing hiking gear, and barefoot Western girls in Tibetan tunics. Dozens of Indian men served tea and wiped tables or sat idly at the cafés, watching the traffic on the road.

As I took in those first sights and sounds, I had no way of knowing how the weeks that stretched ahead would change me, and how I would find a place in that world. Besides the long sessions and Buddhist practice that began the second day, I learned life lessons among those fellow travelers. I joined the ranks of the sidewalk cafés. Hundreds of times I crisscrossed those alleyways and streets between our guest house and the monastery where we studied, and the restaurants where we ate our second dinners late at night and where I learned to drink beer. I came to know that many of those world travelers were admirers of the Dalai Lama, Buddhist practitioners, but most of all wanderers and seekers of the transcendent Buddha-nature within. There were Indians, Australians, Brits, Swedes, Americans, Israelis, Japanese, a certain type from any corner of the world might end up there.

My time in Dharamsala was full of discovery. The very air taught my brain new ways of seeing. But I was there with a singular purpose—to start my journey as a bodhisattva.

DURING THAT MONTH-LONG trip to Dharamsala, I received the teaching on the forty-seven verses of the bodhisattva.

"Come look out this window," the Dalai Lama instructed, looking down on the green lawns surrounding the Namgyal Monastery.

A dozen young monks, all with shaved heads and crimson robes tucked into their belts, ran back and forth chasing a soccer ball. We watched as two monks dashed headlong at each other, the ball flying off the head of one, their bodies momentarily bouncing off each other, the briefest of collisions and then feet once again flying over ground.

"What are they doing?" the Dalai Lama asked. "Tell me what you see them doing."

Another American student, a man in his forties named Jenga, gamely said, "Playing soccer?"

"That is what we see them doing. But is it possible one of them might have *bodhicitta* mind?"

In a voice that sounded unused, Longo ventured, "Clear of earthly thoughts."

"Yes! Now I'll tell you something that I've learned." The Dalai Lama placed a hand on Longo's shoulder and then pointed at me as well.

"At first, you find your practice where you find it. And it may likely be in motion. Running, walking, soccer might be just the right thing for emptying your mind. Eventually, you will cultivate a sitting practice. Meditating while still—still body, still mind. But your youth may require a running practice!"

He looked at Longo and added, "Play football or swim. But meditate and do not choose to suffer."

The Dalai Lama reached for a gong that was beside him. He picked up a padded drumstick and struck the gong in a series of deep tones. The more I listened, and the more I became submerged in the sound, the more human the sound became. As the vibrations of the last gong died out, he patted his knees, requesting each of us to shift into lotus position on our cushion.

He began a chant of *Om* that reverberated around the room, making our five voices into one. The more I listened to our synchronized voices, and the more I became submerged in the sound, the more we sounded like a gong.

After the final *Om* faded in the air, the Dalai Lama continued.

"Human life is impermanent. You only need to think of your loved ones and acquaintances who have died to have proof of the ever-present reality of our impermanent nature. The aspect of death that terrifies us most is that suddenly we are all alone."

For most my childhood, alone meant being just with Jamie, alone with my twin. But when I found the Dalai Lama and my practice, alone suddenly meant without Jamie.

I pictured Jamie the day of her near-drowning, standing in my uncle's guest room in her bathing suit, her eyes on me, hurt. I realized I feared death more than anything, my own but even more so, Jamie's.

As though my fear had been voiced out loud, the Dalai Lama answered.

"No one and nothing leaves this world with us, except for our spiritual practice. We benefit from the existence of the enlightened ones. They are our teachers and friends along the way."

With the words *teacher* and *friend,* His Holiness patted his own chest, naming himself as these relationships to us.

"Spiritual practice is your path. It is the only thing you will take with you."

After our lesson, I walked beside Longo from the bottom steps of the Namgyal monastery down the foothill of Meru Mountain. When we hit a dirt path heading down through the mist, Longo broke into a run. I watched him run away from me, and then I took off after him. I ran full tilt with legs that succumbed to gravity, that were loose-jointed and wild as a colt's. My arms pumped and wind-milled to keep my balance, to keep me from crashing. I sucked in huge breaths and exhaled crazy laughter. The dirt path joined up with a cobblestone street as we entered the town of Dharamsala. We ran on, side by side, thundering all the way to the red wooden door of our guest house.

Longo and I both doubled over holding our knees as we tried to catch our breath. As my breathing came back to normal, I said to Longo, "Is samsara always suffering?"

Still bent over, facing the ground, Longo raised his eyes to look at me. "Uncontrollably recurring rebirth?" he said, his tone implying, *Doesn't that sound like hell to you?*

I imagined those births around the world, infant after infant crying his way into existence. Never-ending life without enlightenment.

"But are people always suffering?"

Longo straightened, his breath suddenly quiet. "Without Dharma understanding, life is an endless cycle of suffering. We helplessly move from one life to the next without meaning, always wanting, unable to create our own peace of mind, unable to look inward."

Longo paused and looked at me. "Some believe that one creates his next world on the way to enlightenment."

My mind drew a blank at these words.

"When your world is starting to collapse," Longo continued, "as your death approaches, you will create a new world and move into it."

We were surrounded by dollhouse-like wooden homes and shops. It had begun raining while we stood there. Dripping worn-out prayer flags were strung back and forth across the alley, and at the end of our quiet street, an ever-present stream of people walked to and fro. Tibetan and Hindi voices were as present in the air as the rain and mist.

I laughed nervously. "I might have created this world?"

Longo shrugged indifferently. "Some also believe that while you are changing bodies and worlds, like changing your jacket from one to another, you encounter the others who are on the same spiritual path you are on. And the world you created, if you did, bumps up against the worlds of those on a similar path. Worlds with karmic threads that connect them."

I imagined myself in a previous world, one that didn't have continents separated by oceans, didn't have skyscrapers, busses, or planes, didn't speak in multitudes of languages, or manufacture passports or flags, or currencies, or even have religions and governments.

And I imagined Jamie in a different world still. Her world was thick with forests, animals, and rivers, where everyone made things with their hands and knew infinite crafts, creating from scratch everything they wore and used.

My world and Jamie's world had threads joining them, as plentiful as a spider's web, keeping them in parallel paths for eternity, putting us into the same womb in the next world and the next.

"David, you don't *see* the suffering. That's what's stopping you."

Before I could answer him, Longo pushed open the wooden door of our guest house and disappeared inside. It wouldn't have mattered if he'd remained. I was speechless.

Chapter 7

Jamila

I FED TOKENS into the machine and selected "Slow Balls." We'd been on countless trips to Coney Island, the two of us swinging bats in adjacent cages, David's twenty automated pitches always finishing a good minute before mine. In our prime, neither of us missed a ball. But that Saturday of my thirtieth year, I missed ball after ball, swinging crazily as each ball propelled toward me.

David cried out, "Eyes open, Jamila!" in time for my last ball. A stunning crack of the bat, and the ball soared out into the net.

David dropped tokens in for his set. He looked lean and somewhat frenzied, with his overgrown buzz cut poking out in every direction. His waist swiveled as he hit pitch after pitch, not missing a one, the bat and ball exploding with each contact.

I realized that for the first time since taking the pills, I was happy. The boardwalk, the warming sun, our ride on the Ferris wheel with its view of the beach and toy-sized roller coaster, but most of all David's company held my sorrow at a distance. We walked on the worn-wood boardwalk toward Brighton Beach, a long walk without speaking, like the elderly Russian couples who strolled, arm-in-arm, nothing left to say after decades of marriage. David steered me over to the metal railing where we faced the gray sea.

"Jamie, Mom and Dad don't know what happened?"

I'd deliberated about this while I was in the hospital. There'd never been any choice about them knowing what I'd done before; I was a child. In the last few days I'd grown determined that they would never know about this one.

"They can't support you if you keep it secret."

"David, please don't tell them. If I have to, I will, but let me do it."

"I need to tell them I'm here. The monastery in Tibet called Mom."

"I know. Can you tell them you're here, but not why? Please."

"Yeah. I won't say anything."

The small waves crashed repeatedly. The beach was crowded with end of summer beach goers getting in the last of the season. It was September, a time of new beginnings.

"Salam is married. That's how I know we've broken up. He has a wife."

"What?" David turned to me with a look of disdain. "You guys were cheating?"

"Technically only he was, I think. He was here alone. I didn't know he was married. He just told me a few days ago. She's here now, in New York."

David scanned the horizon, processing the full story, I guessed.

"So you found out he was married and you took a bottle sleeping pills."

I watched the seagulls pick at food scraps in the sand and dive into garbage cans. They were self-interest machines. "I found out I couldn't be with him anymore and I wanted to die."

David turned toward me and grabbed my chin. I thought of those baseballs cracking against his bat, the power behind them. "Don't say that!" he hissed.

"Don't say what?" Tears filled my eyes and rolled down my cheeks.

David let go of my face. "I never thought you really wanted to die. None of the times."

I turned and raised myself onto the metal railing, my back to the beach, hooking my feet through the lower bar. David automatically copied my movements; our bodies held identical positions, like shadows.

MY PARENTS QUICKLY found a child psychologist after my first incident, in the pool. Anne was Jungian, like both my parents, but younger than them. She wore bell-bottom jeans with a brown leather belt.

I sat on a yellow-and-blue floral couch, and Anne sat in an armchair across from me. There were various objects on the table between us.

"You can touch any of those," Anne said, "That's what they're here for. A lot of people like to move their hands while they think and talk."

I picked up a huge metal nail that must have weighed three pounds. "Is this from a railroad?"

"Yes, from the tracks. I found it."

I held the railroad tie in my lap and looked into Anne's face for the first time. Dark freckles were scattered across her cheeks like constellations. She had long wheat-colored hair.

I barely spoke at all for the first two appointments, and yet each time Anne declared it a good visit to my mom in the waiting room when the hour was up.

On the third appointment, Anne asked me what things I enjoyed doing.

"I like to read. And I knit."

"You can bring your knitting here if you want," she said, to my surprise. "What are you reading now?"

"*The Diary of Anne Frank,*" I said. I'd chosen it because of the name Anne, her name, but I didn't tell her that.

"That's a mature book for a ten-year-old. Do you find it sad?"

"No. I feel bad that she died, but how she talked wasn't sad. It was . . . energetic."

Anne laughed. She was plain-looking but turned beautiful when she smiled. "She was a lively girl."

I fell silent again. I thought Anne would fill the silence the way my mother did whenever I was quiet for a moment, but she just waited for me.

"My family thinks I'm gloomy. I'm not. I enjoy things. But I'm not that bubbly."

"There's no need to be bubbly. What's important is how you feel."

"It's weird that if you planned something, it's called premeditated," I blurted out.

Anne seemed to think through what I'd said. "Why's that weird?" She pushed her hair back behind her shoulders. I decided I wanted my hair to be as long as hers.

"Meditation is a good thing. It's something special that's hard to do. My brother is a Buddhist, and he meditates. But premeditation is such a bad thing."

My parents had made a big deal of this after the pool incident—that my behavior was not premeditated.

"I see. Usually, premeditation is used to talk about planning ahead to do something harmful." Anne placed one ankle on her opposite knee instead of crossing her legs like my mom. "I heard about your brother from your mom. You're twins, yes?"

"Yeah."

"And he's a Buddhist."

"He was born with an enlightened soul."

"What does that mean?"

I turned the railroad tie in my hands, brushed its rusty sides with my fingertips. "Can I ask you something?"

"Yes."

"Since we're twins, is it possible we have only one soul . . . and David has it?"

Anne's face was pained for an instant, like she'd jammed her toe. She leaned in toward me. "I'm looking at you right now, looking in your eyes, Jamie, and I can tell you—you have a soul."

I wiped away tears with my sleeve.

"You want to know what I think, Jamie?"

I didn't say yes or no.

"I don't think you're gloomy. I think you have a lot to deal with, and you're a smart and serious girl who really thinks about things."

I looked away, hiding a smile.

WE RODE THE subway home from Coney Island and walked down Union Street toward my apartment. At my local fire station stood a life-size wooden sculpture of two firemen forming a pyramid, raising an American flag. At the base of the sculpture, amidst the firemen's wooden boots lay bouquets of fresh flowers.

David and I stopped walking and looked.

"What day is it?" I asked.

"I don't know," David said.

The firehouse gate was raised, and inside people clustered together around long tables covered with food.

At the same time, my brother and I said, "It's 9/11."

I looked away from the families inside the station and back at the bouquets they'd brought every year since *the* 9/11. David had been in Dharamsala. I remember we'd spoken; he'd called.

"For weeks afterwards there were flyers taped up here, Missing persons flyers. Photos of strong, young men with their wife or girlfriend pressed against their side. Firemen, who usually do the finding, were the ones missing."

I imagined what those days had been like for the people who went out in the night that followed to post fliers for their unreturned loved ones. I had watched the towers fall from my rooftop in Brooklyn. In horror, I saw people jump out of windows to escape the flames, their bodies tiny as ants.

My brother seemed far away, with his eyes glued on the memorial, his hands limp at his sides.

"Let's get home." I picked up his hand and led him.

Back inside my apartment, David was still rather despondent when his cellphone rang. He yelped when he saw it was the Dalai Lama. His whole demeanor changed. He glowed brighter, as though a dimmer switch had been raised all the way up. I left him alone to speak to his beloved teacher.

Circling my apartment restlessly, I was aware that the wolf was gone. The air was cleared of her. David had gone through something hard in Tibet. I didn't know exactly what, but he'd said enough for me to know his trip had not gone well and from what I heard of his conversation with the Dalai Lama, their bond was tested too. Yet, there are people in life who just make us burn brighter, who we love without reason or explanation, and it was folly to deny them. As I walked around my place my thoughts turned to Salam and some previously unknown empowerment came over me.

When I heard David hang up, I entered the kitchen. His joyous expression made me smile too.

"The Dalai Lama called you."

"Yeah. I'm so relieved."

"What did he say?"

"He's coming to America and he'd like my help during his visit."

"That's great!" I wondered if David might stay awhile. Suddenly there were brighter possibilities everywhere.

"David, I'm going to go see Salam."

David slowly came back into the room, his face going from dreamy to agitated. "You can't. His wife is here. It's over."

"I know, but Chitra said he's sick. I need to find out what that means. I have to see him again, even if just to say goodbye."

"He knows how to reach you. Don't go over there."

Although I was seeking his approval, or even permission, it angered me that David acted like he could call the shots.

"What do you know? You don't have human relationships like the rest of us. You swoop in here and think you can say what I can and can't do."

David's eyes flared with emotion matching my own. "Exactly! You hurt yourself and then I'm supposed to come running. And it's still my fault."

Tears sprang to my eyes. He was right about our dynamic. Our family had created the mythology over the years. His path was what caused me pain and only he could comfort me. I heard myself breathing, like the wolf's panting, but not her, just me.

"David, it's not your fault." Those words were strangely comforting and new. "I'm not your fault."

David stopped short and gave me a long look. "I'm going with you."

WHEN WE ARRIVED at Salam's, I stared up at the building, unsure I could go through with it. Salam's windows faced the street. The curtains, which I'd only noticed from the inside, always parted to both sides, were drawn closed.

"You ready?" David asked.

I rang Salam's buzzer.

A minute passed before Chitra's cautious response came. "Who is it?"

"It's Jamila."

There was a long moment of silence before we heard her voice again. "Wait there. I'll tell Salam you're here."

David murmured a dubious sound but didn't say anything.

The intercom crackled alive again. "Come in." The door buzzed coldly.

Chitra was waiting in the hallway with their apartment door shut behind her. Her hair was pulled into a long ponytail, and she wore a white tee-shirt over narrow black jeans. She was unadorned and beautiful.

David stuck out his hand. "Hi, I'm Jamie's brother, David."

Her arms stayed at her sides. "I'm Chitra."

I cleared my throat, unsure what to say about why we were there.

Chitra didn't hesitate. "Salam would like to see you, but he wants me to tell you something first. You can come in." She turned and went inside, leaving the door open behind her.

Motioning that David and I should take the couch, Chitra sat in a chair facing us. I looked around the room for changes since her arrival, clues that my place here was gone. Salam and I had lain on the same couch for hours, reading the newspaper, sipping coffee, or with Salam's face nestled between my legs, or his penis growing soft and spent against my belly. I'd stood in the kitchen, still as a statue, while Salam spoke to Chitra on the phone in a language I couldn't understand. From where I sat, I saw a red tablecloth on the kitchen table that hadn't been there before.

"Salam has leukemia. He was diagnosed two years ago. Treatment had very little effect. He wanted to live in America before he died. It was something he always dreamed of."

My heart stopped. At first, I thought she was telling me he was dead, but then I remembered she said I could see him.

Chitra studied me, but I knew my face contained no reaction for her to read. I was numb and must have worn a blank expression.

It must have been plain to see that neither of us was going to make a move. David broke the tension, saying, "Perhaps Jamie could go in and see him."

Chitra nodded, holding his gaze while she spoke to me. "He's awake and expecting you. He runs out of energy fast."

When I cracked open their bedroom door and peered into the dim room, I felt I knew the place well, but as if from another lifetime. There was a new heavy curtain covering the window. A folding table near the bed contained a tray with a half-eaten bowl of soup atop it and countless prescription bottles. My mind flashed to my own emptied prescription bottle, still lying on my bathroom floor. I closed the door and leaned against it, not moving toward him. Salam was propped up against the pillows. His silky hair looked dull. With only his face and shoulders in view, I could still see he was thinner. Salam smiled at me with shining eyes.

He looked exactly like a patient, Chitra's patient.

I covered my mouth with my hand and whispered, "Oh my god. This is insane. What am I supposed to say to your wife when she tells me, 'He's expecting you' . . . 'his energy fades fast'? What am I supposed to say to you?"

Salam frowned. "Please come here and sit down."

"Your energy didn't fade ten days ago—you were the picture of health." My voice rose desperately. Had he glimpsed me stalking like the wolf, licking up the pills, I would have been equally unrecognizable to him.

"A lot of my energy went into being with you. Have you ever heard of being able to turn on for something important and otherwise being a train wreck?"

I had firsthand experience of exactly that.

"Jamie, it was undoubtedly selfish of me to enjoy all those days and nights with you and not tell you I was sick. It was a gift to myself. And when you're not angry anymore, and I'm long gone, you might look at it that way too." He took a deep breath, exhausted by his speech. "I really hope so."

I stepped closer to the bed.

"This past week, I've said to myself a thousand times, *he's married.* I kept imagining you growing old with her, your hair still thick and silky, but gray. I pictured you wearing glasses with clunky frames, a cardigan sweater, your dignified and still-beautiful wife by your side, grandchildren to give candy and video games to."

"You're not lifting my spirits. But I guess you know that."

I sat at the foot of the bed. "Salam, I'm so sorry. I can't believe you're really sick! I don't understand it."

"How could you? You just found out."

"I've thought of nothing but the fact that you're married. And I've been so mad at you." I covered my face with my hands. "Are you going to die?"

"Yes."

I wept, hiding behind my hands. "I'm sorry. I'm no good today."

"You don't have to be good, angel."

I wiped away my tears and finally looked at him. Slowly, Salam moved over in bed and made a space for me to rest beside him. We lay there without speaking. Salam scooted lower in bed, rested his head on my shoulder, and wrapped his arm around my waist.

He was married. He was dying. These things were now known and could never be taken back. They were part of the universe. But so was his weight resting on me and the familiar almond scent of him. I stroked his hair from his forehead to the nape of his neck. That he still cared for me was part of the universe now too.

Salam's breathing slowed and his body grew heavier. He had fallen asleep. I slid out from under him, straightened the blanket around his body, and crept off the bed. I kissed the seashell of his ear without making a sound.

WHEN DAVID WENT on his first Buddhist retreat when we were ten years old, it was Grandma who I needed. Something had skipped a generation to connect Grandma and me. With my mother anchored between us, at times exerting her control over each of us, we clung together giddily like a pair of fast friends. We shared our love of animals and the ability to make almost anything with our hands. At the end of my first week without my twin, I called my grandma to ask if I could stay with her for the weekend.

"You're always welcome here. I think there's a parade in Chinatown this week too. You know Grandma lives in Chinatown now?"

This "now" was a joke, because Grandma hadn't moved in fifty years, but Chinatown had moved in around her.

"Is your mother home? Put her on and I'll see if I can come get you."

After my mom picked up in her room, I pretended to hang up the kitchen phone, but stayed on the line listening to their call.

"Let me take Jamie for the weekend, give you and Leonard a break."

"Did she call you?"

"Is that a crime?" Grandma responded

"Of course not. We don't really need a break, especially with David gone already."

"Hmm." Grandma's famous hum.

"Does she need a break from us?"

"I'm sure she's very happy having all your attention. You know how we love spending time together."

"She can come down there for the weekend if that's what you both want."

"Great! I'll take the train up there and get her."

"Okay, Ma." My mother sighed, a world-weary sound I'd grown to know.

"What's the matter, darling?" Grandma asked.

"Everything's fine. I'm just not surprised Jamie wants to get out of here and come be with you. It's all topsy-turvy in this house. I do my best with the twins and I love them very much, and still David may never fit into society, and Jamie is living under a dark cloud."

A dark cloud? I gently put the phone down in the cradle and looked at the ceiling above me. I pictured a black storm cloud opening up and rain falling down on me.

The weekend at Grandma's provided all the usual comforts, with many games of checkers and chess, her showing me how to knit and do needlework, eating her Jewish cooking, but I also worried about the things I'd heard my mom say about me. There was something brewing in me, something like storm clouds. I didn't want to be the one who was eclipsing the sun, but I didn't know how to be any other way.

I'D CANCELLED MY weekly dinner with Grandma two weeks in a row, since taking the pills and spending several days at Bellevue Hospital and since David had arrived. Although I was tempted to hide from her, I didn't want to miss another week.

When I opened her front door, yelling, "Grandma, I'm here," I was faced by a football-player-sized woman with a dishtowel draped over her shoulder. I screamed, thinking I'd somehow walked into the wrong apartment, or worse, stepped into the future, after Grandma died. The beloved smells of Grandma's place were all there though and I could see her china cabinet and ancient rugs.

"Sorry to scare you, young lady. I'm Bethany, Lill's helper." She patted my shoulder.

"Hi. I forgot Grandma had a helper." I smiled sheepishly. "How's it going?"

"Oh, Bethany does alright." She chuckled. "Oh, no, your grandma got me talking like she does—calling myself by my own name. She's in her bedroom, just took a shower. Go see if you can rub Ben-Gay on her shoulder. She won't let me."

I called out to Grandma from outside her closed bedroom door.

"Oh, you're here!" She pulled her bedroom door open. Grandma's eyes bore into mine. "Jamie, what happened?" Her vision was like a mother toward her infant, able to see fatigue or hunger, fear or curiosity when others saw only a baby. My face told her some story.

"Nothing happened." We clasped each other in an embrace, Grandma humming appreciatively. I kissed her head, which only came up to my chin, fighting the sudden urge to cry.

Her mostly black hair was wet and neatly parted down the middle, with short bangs that she cut herself. Grandma was wearing one of five blouses that I knew by heart, a seventies polyester shock of neon pinks and oranges.

"Grandma, can I rub some Ben-Gay on your shoulder? Is it hurting today?"

"Oh, that's okay, Grandma's all dressed now." She reached awkwardly with her left hand over her right shoulder and pressed her bony fingers into the sore spot. "I put some on after my shower already." She winced.

"I don't believe you. Come here, let me smell you. I'll be able to smell if you're telling the truth." I stuck my nose in the collar of her blouse and sniffed deeply. "Grandma's lying! I smell only Ivory soap, no Ben-Gay."

Grandma giggled like a girl. "You don't want to rub these old bones," she said suggestively, and I knew she'd let me.

"Take off your blouse and lie down. I'll rub it for ten minutes, and you will feel so much better."

While I rubbed the mentholated cream into her back, I felt that I was stroking my future body. Her bird-like bones and thin skin were soft and lovely to me. She murmured with relief.

I imagined telling her I was deeply in love with a man named Salam, but that he was married to someone else. If I told her I had a friend sick with leukemia, she'd tisk her tongue sympathetically. And if I said I'd taken sleeping pills, that I'd hurt myself again, she'd leap off the bed ready to defend me, even from myself. But none of these utterances were possible.

I made circular sweeping motions on her back to end the massage.

"You're all done, Grandma."

She tugged her blouse back on. "Hmm, much better. Grandma doesn't need anything now . . . except her granddaughter."

We made our way down the hall to the kitchen.

"Oh, Bethany, it's shining in here," Grandma cheered. "And you got those dishes up in that cupboard. How did you reach?"

"You see how tall I am. I'm not a tiny thing like you." She towered over my grandmother by about a foot and a half. "It's time for me to cut out. You all set?"

"Oh, yes, I'm going to make dinner for my little girl here."

When we finished eating, we moved to Grandma's living room.

"Are you making anything now?" Grandma asked.

"Knitting?"

"Yes. It helps take your mind off things." She raised an eyebrow at me, probing.

"Not right now."

"Come see if you like any of Grandma's yarns. You'll start something."

Start something.

I chose a large roll of indigo blue that Grandma had in her cupboard and asked her for a round needle to make a hat. We settled on the couch, both of us with yarn in our laps.

She said, "Let me tell you a story about me and about your mom too."

"Go right ahead." I was enjoying the clicking motion of Grandma's aluminum needles in my hands. I hadn't knit anything in a long time, yet I could still look at Grandma and let my fingers work on their own.

"I was nineteen when your grandfather, Will, asked me to marry him. Will was a self-educated, self-made chemist working for DuPont for ten dollars a week. He was also a Communist. We went with his friend and comrade, Dan, to City Hall to be witnesses to Dan's marriage. Will turned to me and said, 'Let's get married too. I'll get you out of that house.' So we did."

A perfect little circle of knitted yarn had formed in my hands. I settled in to my work while I listened.

"I didn't get out of that house so easily though. I was too scared to tell my parents what I'd done. Weeks later, I confided in my mother that I'd gotten married to Will. My mother grieved, 'Why? Your sisters will be shamed! The older ones must marry before the younger. I have a hope chest for Menucha, nothing for you!' After hours of beating her chest, it occurred to my ma that I couldn't have gotten married—the Rabbi knew they were trying to find a match for my sister Menucha, who was already twenty-three."

Grandma scowled, squinting her eyes and jutting her chin, to imitate her mother.

"'Where's your *katuba*?' she demanded. 'You went to the Rabbi?'

"'No, Ma, we were married at City Hall.'

"My mother waved the air with relief, 'City Hall! That doesn't mean anything. Get dressed. We're going to see the Rabbi.'

"My ma listened, crestfallen, to her rabbi. Not married Jewish, but married in America, legally married. To her it was meaningless, but she feared and respected the state. She would have to tell my father. Menucha would be shamed. And I would have to move out and live with my new husband. I left that house with nothing but the clothes on my back."

Grandma had told me before how she left home with absolutely nothing. It always gave her some proud satisfaction.

"Look at you. You'll finish that hat before I finish my story."

I followed Grandma's gaze to my hands. The yarn was thick, already a small bowl.

"That will make a lovely present for a gentleman."

She was probing once again. "Go on, Grandma. I'm listening."

"Okay, well, Will put me off for a number of years about children. At first it was easy to say no. Together, we earned twenty-five dollars a week. We shared a one-bedroom apartment with Dan and his wife. But eventually, as the years wore on, and we moved into our own apartment, Will finally admitted he was afraid to have children. He was afraid they would be raised in an orphanage like he was. 'They'll have us! We'll be their caregivers,' I told him. I promised that even if he died I would never put our children in an orphanage. He gave in."

Grandma paused. She ended a row on her blanket and moved the yarn off the needle to start again. There was a solemn air about her that I was unaccustomed to.

"I became pregnant for the first time at twenty-eight. I survived morning sickness with joy. I even admired my swollen legs. Then, in the second trimester, I lost the baby."

"I'm sorry, Grandma." I already knew that Grandma had suffered a late miscarriage before my mother.

"Okay. Well, I became pregnant again two months later. I was twenty-nine, fearfully old at the time. I carried myself around like a glass vase. My belly swelled five, six, and seven months. Very good. I breathed only slightly easier though, and I prayed to the moon. Will waited on me at home in the evenings, but I worked full time as a shipping secretary, saving money for the baby. Labor began as it should, right at nine months. I labored in this apartment, attended by a midwife and my mother and older sister, Menucha. For two straight days, I labored. Will went to work on the second day, then poor, scared Will spent the night sleeping on that couch." Grandma pointed to where I sat. "A woman's place this house was. Finally, in the early hours, I delivered my baby girl. She was perfectly formed . . . but dead."

"Oh, Grandma! That's terrible. I thought you were talking about Mom's birth." I stopped knitting and put the needles down next to me. My grandfather had lain right where I was sitting while his unborn daughter had died in the womb.

"It nearly killed me. I'm telling you for a reason though. I was through with life after that. I lost my will to have a baby and to live. We named her Melody and buried her in a tiny grave."

I pictured this baby girl who was never given a chance at life, an alternate version of my own mother.

"At thirty, I became pregnant with your mom. For half the pregnancy I moped around, crying and waiting for the loss. Then one day I woke up feeling the insistent kicks. I leapt out of bed overjoyed. 'Will, I never felt Melody kick strong like this! This baby is hungry and wants to live. This baby is going to live!'

"From that day on, I got ready for your mom's arrival. Pure hopefulness. And finally I got your mother, a beautiful healthy baby." Grandma smiled, like clouds parting.

I wiped away my tears.

"Sometimes I like to tell myself I had two little girls, Melody and Margot. But truly, Melody went on to live somewhere else, or maybe she jumped right into Margot to come back to me." Grandma lifted one shoulder coquettishly.

"You believe in reincarnation?"

"Oh, that word. I don't know about that. That's a David word. But souls must go somewhere. Only bodies go in the ground."

It was nearly impossible for me to think that perished bodies were not the ultimate loss.

The conversation brought back a memory. "I used to worry that twins were born with one soul and that David had ours."

"No, the opposite." Grandma stilled her needles in an X. "Twins provide a great opportunity. When there are two people who love each other very dearly, inseparably, they look for a pair of twins, so they can reenter the world together."

Chapter 8

David

JAMIE AND I had just returned home from Coney Island. I was hungry and tired, my skin grimy from sweat and the muggy salt air. We entered her apartment, comfortably silent together, just like when we were kids returning home from school, hungry and tired, ready to fill up on snacks and watch TV, not needing to speak.

I drank a glass of water while standing at her kitchen sink and then refilled the glass and handed it to Jamie. My cell phone, which was usually not even turned on, rang.

"His Holiness" appeared on my phone's face in a green glow.

"It's the Dalai Lama." I clutched the phone to my ear. "Your Holiness. Hello."

His voice came through as clear as if he were in the same room with me.

"David, dear boy, greetings to you."

The strength I'd managed those last few days, since leaving Tibet, was swept away. I needed him like a baby needs its mother.

"Your Holiness, it's really you. I've been holding you very near."

"So you know what's happened there?" he asked. "I wasn't sure if the news would make its way into the monastery."

The Dalai Lama thought I was still in Tibet. My parents also didn't know I was in New York. I swore to myself that I'd call them right after talking to His Holiness. My heart was racing and my legs shook violently. I revisited the adrenaline-filled energy of my obsessive pursuit of Lobsang. I was no longer in Sichuan Province. I had never entered the monastery or met the esteemed teacher who the highest lama in the world had chosen for me. There was nothing I could do at this point to change those realities. I took a deep breath.

"Your Holiness, I never went to the monastery."

A humming sound rose questioningly over the phone, the sound of an irritated bee. "David, you know there are circumstances conducive to your practice. A spiritual teacher has accepted you."

"I know."

"Tell me, what is the atmosphere there? The young man was in your village, right?"

He'd heard about the new self-immolation; that's why he was calling. I pictured the Dalai Lama seated at his desk in Dharamsala, in the same room where six weeks ago he told me to go study at Kirti in Tibet. His posture would be slightly hunched in his chair, the phone held to his ear, his other hand resting in his lap, peering over his glasses at the window.

"Yes, it happened in my village square. I was there. The police shot him. They killed him, even as he burned." I began crying as I spoke to him. He was the only person I had told.

The Dalai Lama exhaled through his teeth, making a sound over the phone like the hissing of a lion.

He spoke in an unfamiliar voice. "If only I could walk the streets of Tibet with my brothers, as you are." I realized it was anger I heard in his voice.

"Your Holiness," I dreaded speaking these words, "I left Tibet. The same day I saw the self-immolator, I had a flight out. My sister is not well. I came to New York to be with her."

Jamie had been standing beside me when my phone rang. But when she realized it was the Dalai Lama, she'd left the room to give me privacy.

When the Dalai Lama's voice came through the phone again it was stronger, his calm-abiding was restored.

"As it should be perhaps. You are there for your sister. And now I see that I can ask you for the help that I need too. I have made arrangements to come to America. I can never enter my mother country again. My role is to make Tibet known by the rest of the world, for my brothers and sisters in Tibet. I need an organizer for my trip. Would you be that person?"

"Of course—I'd be honored to. Your Holiness, I'm so sorry I let you down in Tibet."

"Maybe you are where you are supposed to be. Maybe you will return to Kirti. But right now Tibetan tradition is endangered. Tibet is becoming a figment, a word. Her traditions are all that keep Tibet in this world. And I, myself may need to tear down Tibetan tradition."

His words brought a chill to my heart. What tradition could he mean?

AFTER TWO WEEKS of study in Dharamsala, we arrived at our classroom in the monastery one morning to find another monk, as solid as a boulder, standing by the window next to the Dalai Lama. As we settled on our cushions on the floor, the Dalai Lama clasped the hand of this monk and, smiling broadly, introduced him to us. "This is my venerable teacher, the great Lama, Dilgo Khyentse Rinpoche."

Dilgo Khyentse Rinpoche was one of the last great Tibetan Lamas to complete his training and studies in Tibet. I loved him at first sight, the same chemistry I'd felt six years earlier, at the age of eight when I first met the Dalai Lama. Dilgo Khyentse Rinpoche's face was as round as the moon, with wide-set deep brown eyes, and a perpetual smile. Like the Dalai Lama, he had a magnetic quality.

He stepped into the circle of students with his hands in prayer pose and bowed slightly to each of us. He appeared as un-moveable as a mountain, his eyes wide with excitement. His charisma filled the small room to the roof beams.

"It is important to appreciate the inconceivable strength and effect a single thought has of benefiting another. When injurious thoughts prevail and people think of nothing but harming each other, the general welfare of the world declines daily. I have come to you with a teaching from the fourteenth century, based on one of the most revered texts of Tibetan Buddhism: *The Thirty-seven Verses on the Practice of the Bodhisattva*. I will be teaching you these verses, and if you choose, you will take the vow of the bodhisattva."

I looked at Longo, his eyes were closed, his back perfectly straight as he sat in lotus pose, and I imagined I saw his readiness. Longo, I thought, further along in his practice and older than me, was better equipped to absorb the Rinpoche's teaching. But I internally rejoiced that I was only fourteen, still a child when I would become a bodhisattva. Close to innocence, I could recognize the unequivocal truth.

"These verses are not words to turn to in an hour of need. They are a way of life, a commitment to a way of seeing and *being*. And they should serve you most when you have forgotten them.

> *Now that I have this great ship, a precious human*
> *life, so hard to obtain,*
> *I must carry myself and others across the ocean of samsara.*
> *To that end, to listen, reflect, and meditate*
> *Day and night, without distraction, is the practice of*
> *A bodhisattva.*

We repeated aloud the first of thirty-seven verses to our teacher. Khyenste loomed over us, his massive chest wrapped in crimson robes, his moon-like face alert. For the next hour, we each said aloud all thirty-seven verses. On our first day at Namgyal Monastery we had been told to memorize the thirty-seven verses. It was the longest memorization of my young life and I thought I couldn't do it. But in those past weeks, I had often stopped along the monastery's walkways to listen to the monks who clustered in small groups, taking turns reciting *sutras*. A stream of Tibetan words would drift heavenward, while a young monk held his gaze locked in the distance, his torso rocking with concentration. An accomplished monk might recite a text from sunup until sundown, a hundred pages memorized.

I knew way back then that I didn't have within me the same stuff that they were made of. It was almost like I could foresee that I would one day fail—even while walking the sacred ground of Dharamsala. But I kept moving forward, ignoring what I already knew.

When each of us had recited the bodhisattva vow, Khyentse held one arm aloft.

"There are necessary advantages conducive to Dharma practice. I want you to know the conducive circumstances you have been given. Given!" His first finger pointed to the heavens. "A Buddha has appeared in the world!"

His second finger sprung from his fist. "Two. He has taught the Dharma!"

Khyentse extended his thumb. "Three. The Dharma has remained and still exists in your time!"

His hand, with only the pinky turned downward, vibrated above his head. "Four. You have entered the Dharma!"

He spread all five fingers taut and slowly rotated his body, showing each of us his extended palm. "Five," he whispered. "You have been accepted by a spiritual teacher."

I glanced at the Dalai Lama, who sat on one side of the room. His eyes were closed, and he wore a tranquil smile. I closed my eyes too, feeling exalted and terrified, in having been accepted by this beloved teacher.

"Will each of you be and remain conducive to the practice? As firm as Mount Meru!" He pointed out the window at the mountain between us and Tibet. My gaze followed and my eyes filled with tears, perhaps sensing my future failures.

"Now listen closely. There are three types of bodhisattvas: the king, the boatman, and the shepherd, each with his own way of being. You will choose your own way."

Khyentse locked eyes with me for an instant. "Or perhaps it is the road that chooses the journeyman."

ONE THING I didn't need explained, didn't need to be taught, but understood upon witnessing was the story of Tibetans in Dharamsala. Every day, at all times, whether it was before dawn, at sun's peak, or in the waning hours of the day, Tibetans were crisscrossing the roads of the Lingkhor—the pilgrim's pathway around the base of the hill where the Dalai Lama lived. I was able to decipher who was Tibetan immediately by their Himalayan features, their tunics, the traditional braids of the women, the caps and trousers of the men, the short pants and sandaled feet of the children. I observed Tibetans of all ages reciting sutras as well-wishes for the long life of the Dalai Lama, or to fortify His Holiness' health and well-being, they hung Tibetan prayer flags on any available perch and across the roadways, and constantly burned dried juniper and threw handfuls of barley for good blessings—to honor their spiritual leader in the way they were forbidden to live in Tibet.

Wherever the Dalai Lama was in body became at once a sacred place and a true home of Tibetans. Tibetans made their home in Dharamsala with the joy of knowing that His Holiness' presence was their Tibet, their dharma, and their home, in the form of a single man.

The day I was to leave Dharamsala and head home, having taken the vow of the bodhisattva at the age of fourteen, I witnessed a scene I will never forget. The Dalai Lama came to Longo and me and said, "Come, my new bodhisattvas, come see a very important part of being the Dalai Lama. Follow me."

We entered a room in the monastery that I'd never seen before. Inside was a group of Tibetan pilgrims. Upon seeing His

Holiness, the women, in braids and dirty red tunics, fell to their knees, shook their heads, and bawled. The men gnashed their teeth, bit their fists, and cried with open mouths and running noses. The elders wrapped their arms around themselves and rocked, doubled over with cries. Their joy was intertwined with their grief. Only the children leapt with their rejoicing. They jumped and caught the Dalai Lama's arms, his robes, yelling in Tibetan, "We've come for you!"

The Dalai Lama moved through the room with his arms extended. Palpable love emanated from the Dalai Lama's body toward his countrymen. They had risked their lives and spent weeks or months bearing the elements to touch this man, and they were rendered speechless.

I looked over at Longo. His mouth was open in astonishment, mirroring the same awe I felt.

It was the first time I ever saw the Dalai Lama weep. He moved slowly from person to person, embracing everyone in the room with his eyes closed and a tear-streaked face. He listened to the utterances that his countrymen offered. He stayed until each person was spent.

After every pilgrim had been embraced and blessed on their journey, His Holiness ushered Longo and me out of the room.

His eyes still wet, he said, "Every month, I greet the recent arrivals from Tibet who have come to see me and to see that somewhere *Tibet* exists freely. Many of them will turn around and go home now."

The Dalai Lama wiped his face with his hands.

"Take a lesson from my countrymen. Everything is shared. Of everything, especially love, there is enough. Every one of the people in that room has been my mother in another lifetime."

I OVERRODE MY misgivings, and the day after our trip to Coney Island, Jamie and I took the subway into Manhattan to try to see Salam. Stepping into Salam and Chitra's apartment, I smelled the familiar odors of Indian spices—cardamom, anise, cumin, and coriander—but underneath it the acrid smell of illness. Their living room consisted of the spare furnishings of someone living temporarily in a foreign country, a lifestyle I knew well myself.

From Jamie's strained body language, I knew the one closed door must be the bedroom where Salam lay sick. I was acutely aware of Salam's presence and the magnetic pull he wielded on Jamie. In his apartment, I could feel the pain he'd caused my sister and the suffering he'd inflicted on his wife, who glared at us.

Chitra told us to sit, and she perched on a chair across from us.

"Salam wants me to tell you that he has leukemia. He's known for two years. It's beyond treatment."

Jamie's face showed almost nothing, a flinch, a mere flicker that as her twin, was enough for me to know she'd been decimated. She seemed unable to utter a word.

"Perhaps Jamie could go in and see him. We don't need to stay long."

Chitra nodded her consent. All three of us stood, and Jamie hurried to his door. She opened it just wide enough for her body to pass through and closed the door behind her.

Chitra left me standing there and went to the kitchen. She returned with two glasses of water. We sat on the couch in silence, like two people in a doctor's waiting room.

"Are you wondering why I let her in today?"

I shook my head no, but she went on.

"He asked me to. And I didn't want to deny him a dying wish. Our marriage was arranged. We were strangers when we got married, but we were starting to grow affectionate toward each other and then he was diagnosed. He asked me to allow this separation. He wanted to fulfil a dream of his, to live in New York."

Chitra seemed too rational. I sensed that was how she wanted to be seen. And the fact that Salam didn't tell Jamie he was sick, or married didn't fit into Chitra's tidy picture.

As if she were responding to my unspoken skepticism, Chitra continued, "A widow not yet thirty can remarry and start over. He begged me to let him come take this job in New York. He said I'd begin to live without him before I had to spend a widow's year in mourning."

Without seeing Salam, I felt his power. The apartment and the women in it existed because of this man's strong will.

Chitra turned to look at the closed bedroom door. I studied her profile, the curve of her forehead, her sharp and delicate face. She seemed like a force to be reckoned with too.

She kept going. "Salam even chose a classmate and friend of mine as a potential new husband for me. This wasn't serious, but I agreed with him that Amir could be a suitable husband. Salam and I soothed each other with this kind of talk, and we became less like husband and wife."

"I'm not sure I'm the person you should be telling this to."

Chitra cut her eyes in my direction. "He came here, and he brought all the love that should have been between us, like a trunk full of clothes, and unpacked it with your sister."

I saw how her distance from her marriage and her strident possessiveness of her husband coexisted. "That's what I mean; I'm her brother. I'm really sorry."

Chitra examined the end of her long ponytail, its straight hairs splayed out like the bristles of a paintbrush.

"Salam told me that Jamila's twin brother was an advanced Buddhist, like a monk." She looked at me. "Are you?"

"I'm a student, a practitioner. Not a monk."

Chitra gave me a skeptical look. "And the Dalai Lama is a friend of yours?"

I had thought of little else since the Dalai Lama's phone call the day before. I was clinging to my connection with him and counting the days until his arrival, and yet it was hard to claim him as my friend in that moment, before this woman who disarmed me.

"He's been one of my teachers."

Chitra raised her eyebrows. "What about Jamila? Is she a Buddhist?"

"No." I laughed. "Not the last time I asked, at least."

"I think she and Salam both operate from a more egocentric philosophy."

I felt the sting of her hurt and anger. My feelings grew embittered too. I wanted to hold Salam responsible for the pain he'd caused to both Chitra and Jamie. But everything I knew about suffering told me to practice universal compassion. And that compassion included my sister and even Salam.

A FEW DAYS later I left Jamie's to go stay with my parents in Manhattan, as I would begin volunteering at the New York City Office of Tibetan Buddhism, organizing the Dalai Lama's American tour immediately.

My mom was going to come home from work to have lunch with me, but I let myself into an empty apartment when I arrived. I went to the kitchen drawer where we'd always kept road maps. I pulled the drawer open and found it exactly the same, stacked with a dozen folded rectangular maps and cluttered with pens, pads, paper clips, pushpins, and all the invariable junk of life.

I hadn't known what to do with my life as the end of high school loomed. When Jamie began her applications, I'd announced that I wasn't going to college. To my surprise, my parents readily accepted this. It seemed they too weren't sure what a bodhisattva did in his adult life. But when Jamie was accepted to Vassar, I decided I better find something to do quickly.

I'd dug through this same kitchen drawer then and pulled out every map of the Northeast and New England. At eighteen, knowing I would leave my parents' home for somewhere, for something, I'd unfolded the maps of the Shenandoah Mountains and the Appalachian Trail and laid them out side by side. My fingers crawled across these maps, following roads and rivers, pausing at lakes and mountains and national parks. My fingers crept south of New York City. Over and over, I found myself gravitating to the large green oblong shape of the Monongahela National Forest.

The next day, at the local library, I learned of a program in forestry that included service learning and a caretaker's cabin right on the edge of Monongahela. My spirits lifted as I prepared to move four hundred miles from my family home, to begin a new phase of life in the national forest.

Once again, twelve years later, I opened the worn creases of the map I knew so well now and allowed my thoughts to drift back into the Monongahela Forest, back into my eighteen-year-old self.

HAVING TAKEN ON the rhythms of the forest, I rose at sunup with the birds. The creaking of tree limbs as the first rays of sun warmed them, or a pinecone hitting the ground were the sounds I heard before I spoke a word. I was a forestry student, a caretaker of the woods and trees, and I tried to live in Dharma wisdom, in wakefulness.

Before handing in my final report of the year, I hiked part of the Appalachian Trail, camping along the route for a week without seeing another human being. During this week, I rose at three a.m. each morning and first chanted and then meditated until the sun rose.

On my last morning, I sat in lotus position on my mat outside my tent and sent blessings to His Holiness, to the bodhisattvas. Then, starting with my eyes, I followed the smoke of balsam incense. My vision grew soft. The movement of the smoke in the air and the movement of my eyes became one fluid natural event.

As though playing a mirror game, my eyes followed the smoke, the smoke followed my eyes.

From my cabin door, it was a quarter-mile walk down a dirt trail to reach the first asphalt road. Five minutes of walking on the paved road brought me to the small park office where I checked in each morning and picked up the maintenance checklists of seasonal chores for the day. Behind the park office was a long field of cut grass that ran downhill, a sloping lawn that ended at a thick stand of spruce, fir, birches, and pines. At the border of the woods, three ginkgos stood guard.

My meditation began with a vision of the ground beneath the three ginkgos, where sun-gold yellow gingko leaves piled high. Each leaf was cool and soft when pressed against my cheek.

The leaves on the ground in their golden pile took on spots of green that grew to streaks, stirring as they filled their veins with oxygen, reversing the deciduous process, the green spread throughout the coarsening leaf. On the momentum of this return to life they, heavily at first and then with agility, rose from the ground and found their original places on the naked gingkos' branches.

Clouds moved through the blue skies in swift time-release motion. The sun and moon accelerated in rotation. And to my surprise, the trees grew younger and younger. The horizontal branches that gave the three gingkos a stiff-armed camaraderie, like three Japanese soldiers, shortened and folded up into the main trunks of their masters. The three trees appeared to sink into the earth, first slowly and then at a faster pace, becoming thinner and thinner.

The gingkos disappeared beneath the earth altogether, beginningless time, and then reemerged in a single breath. Spikes rose quickly through the mulch of pine needles and brown leaves as they sped upward from infancy to stand several feet tall and put forth their first spring buds. As the sky flashed day to night, blue to gray to black, and clouds sped overhead, the gingkos grew back to their full height. Silk leaves emerged, flying through spring and summer like thousands of kites. They yellowed and slipped their way to the ground, thirty times in thirty years, slowed and then came to a complete stop, in the fresh green state in which I knew I'd find them when I made my way down the dirt road and the sloping grassy hill later that morning, heading home.

A blue jay entered the vision, coasting downward on open wings—she landed feather-light on a persimmon branch. I startled and inhaled a deep breath, returning to conscious thought. *Get ready.*

I rolled up my mat and lay it beside my tent. In a matter of minutes, I'd break down my campsite for the last time. But for the moment, I watched the sky.

When I reached my cabin, I opened the three small windows and door and swept the floor of dust and mice droppings. I turned on the faucet in the kitchen and ran the water until it ran clear again. I made a pot of coffee. While the coffee brewed, I stepped out onto my own little patch of grass and lay down in the sun. Automatically, I bent my knees and rose up into wheel pose, reaching my stomach to the sky. As I stretched my spine into a U, I looked at my cabin upside-down. I stayed in wheel until my arms and thighs were quaking. The phone in my cabin, which I'd only heard once or twice since installing it, began ringing. Groaning out loud, I lowered myself down.

It was my mother, and as soon as I said hello she dove in. "It looks like Jamie is dropping out of school. She's been home for three days and has basically done nothing but sleep. She's missing her finals. Where have you been?"

While I listened to my mom, I watched a blue jay hop from spot to spot on the noonday grass, looking for a worm. *You're too late,* I thought. *They're all gone.*

We were eighteen then, our first year of adulthood. And now here I was, a man of thirty, everything I owned fitting in a backpack that rested on the floor beside me, standing here in my socks, looking through the family junk drawer, once again not knowing where I was headed next in life. I pushed the drawer shut, picked up my backpack, and climbed the stairs to my childhood room.

My old lacrosse stick stood in the corner. The walls were painted the same sky blue. On the corkboard above my desk were items I'd pinned to it years earlier. I was startled by a photo of me at age nine, with the Dalai Lama, his hand resting on my head, both of us smiling. There was a chant I'd copied in crayons as a boy, under a scrawled rainbow.

"*Nam Myoho Renge Kyo,*" I said aloud, experimenting with the chant of my younger years.

On my desk sat my old computer that I'd left behind after forestry school. I turned it on and sat down to watch it boot up. I connected to the Internet and Googled "Tibet Self-immolation." For the brief second I waited for what might pop up, I felt the same surge of obsession and compulsion I'd been wrapped in while in Tibet. It could still grab one. I was helpless to resist. It wasn't like I lost my mindfulness, one part of my brain said, this too is the path, everything is used, use it. But another scurrying voice said merely, look for trouble, look for something you don't even want to find.

The first page filled with articles published the week before. I clicked on one from a Lhasa newspaper, and there he was. Not Lobsang, but the man in black. I wondered where in that crowd there had been a photographer, possibly a journalist. If these suicide protests continued, there would be more journalists rushing to Tibet to tell the story of a new epidemic of self-immolation that first appeared in the world in Vietnam in the sixties, and that was deeply antithetical for Buddhists, but happening anyway.

In the photo on the screen, he was very much as I remembered him. He looked like a martial artist, tall and strong, dressed in black. Had he gotten a fresh haircut that morning? I suddenly wanted to know everything he'd done that day, all the while knowing he would take his own life later that same day. *People know about you. I saw you.* Tears streamed down my face as I stared at the screen.

I had been there in Tibet to see this man take his life, but I hadn't chosen to be there. I was content in Dharamsala, beside my first teacher, the highest lama in the land. In that unforeseen moment, when the Dalai Lama told me he would arrange my next teacher in a land he was exiled from, rather than have me stay with him, I'd felt painfully alone, more alone than I could ever remember being.

We had been seated in one of the Dalai Lama's private rooms. The wooden shutters and windows were propped open to the summer air. The soft sound of doves cooing and the sharper calls of loons and hornbills drifted into the room. I also heard wind chimes, distant voices, and the gunning and honking of cars from the road.

Only the blue sky was visible through the nearest window. I watched that square of blue, thinking that if a hornbill crossed through it, I'd take it as a sign. I'd tell His Holiness he was mistaken and that Dharamsala was my home. He was my home. The woven mat beneath our feet gave off the scent of fresh bamboo, and I could smell the eucalyptus and pine trees on the breeze. But no bird passed through that patch of sky.

I walked out of my old room and stood in the open doorway of the bedroom next to mine. Our childhood bedrooms shared a wall and were mirror images of each other. Peering in to Jamie's bedroom, I thought of that terrible spring, when I'd come home from the forest, summoned to pull her out of a dark place.

"Mom, have you tried talking to her?" I asked my mom that late spring from my cabin in Monongahela.

"Yes, in the kitchen at three in the morning; she glared at me and wouldn't speak. I just asked her about school, what she was missing."

"Probably not the best thing to ask her about."

My mother sighed painfully. Then I heard her sniffling. "Mom, are you crying?"

"I'm really scared, David. This is the exact age of the typical onset of major mental illness."

"Slow down, Mom. Jamie's not one of your patients. Maybe she is depressed, but you're there, I'm four hundred miles away. What can I tell you?"

"Do you sense she's not okay?"

"What, in a twin way?"

"Yeah." Mom was openly crying now.

From my cabin doorway, I watched the blue jay tip its head one way and another, looking from ground to tree to midday sun, hungry and coming up empty.

"Do I need to come home?"

"Oh, David. Could you? I know she'll talk to you. If we could just get her back at school, I think she'd be okay."

"Because college is the antidote to mental illness?" I asked bitterly.

"Because you always comfort her."

As I watched, one of the feral cats from the woods crept toward the blue jay. The bird heard or sensed it, but looked in the opposite direction for the danger. "Hold on, Mom." I put the phone down and strode outside.

"Shoo cat! Get out of here!" The bird took off at my voice as the cat leapt through the air, landed on the empty grass, and ran for the trees.

I picked up the phone receiver again. "I'll come home for the weekend, Mom. I'll get there tomorrow evening."

When I got home in the late evening, Jamie was asleep, and I stood in this same spot, outside her room, peering in. The lights were off, but the room glowed with street light through her curtain-less window. I walked over to the bed and stood over my sleeping sister. She wore only a t-shirt and underwear. One knee was bent in a lunge, the other leg stretched long down the bed. I slept this way too.

I saw clearly in the dim light, like train tracks fading into fog, from her knee to the line of her underwear, on the inside of Jamie's thigh she'd carved a series of lines. The scars grew darker, then pinker, then fresher as they travelled up her thigh. The line closest to her underwear had not begun to heal, dry blood surrounded it.

With my index-finger I traced the faintest scar by her knee. She stirred.

"Wake up, Jamie."

From her sleep Jamie responded to my voice. "David?"

I sat on the floor, my back against her bed, facing away. "I'm here."

A moment later, I felt Jamie's hand on top of my head. Other than placing her hand there, she hadn't moved.

We both stayed home for three weeks. I was there, but we both recognized painfully that I resented it. There was something about the track of cuts my twin made up her thigh that felt acutely like an ending. It was like our separation into two distinct people started when I alone saw the colors leave that dead boy's body and I found the Dharma, and Jamie tried to drown herself in the swimming pool. If that was a beginning, I thought the cutting was the ending. Dark and dangerous as it was, it read to me like an acceptance, a line in the sand for her. *We are apart*, that row of cuts said to me.

My mom entered the apartment with a shout that broke my reverie.

"David? Are you here? Where are you?"

"I'm upstairs. I'm coming down."

My mom waited at the bottom of the dark wood staircase and heavy banister, the feel of the curve and grain of that banister which I could conjure in my memory from thousands of trips up and down that staircase, our hands always gliding along the smooth wood.

"Hi, Mama."

She held me in a long embrace, and I felt numerous breaths rise and fall beneath her bony back. Finally, she let me go. "I'm so glad you're okay. Let's go eat."

Our mom never thought to ask how we were. She did all her own narrative-making. And in her narratives, I was always okay and Jamie always wasn't. I'd needed Jamie to point this out to me, but I now knew it to be true.

Mom and I sat at the kitchen table, identical plates of salad, quinoa, and poached eggs in front of us.

"It's so good to have you home, David. But I have to ask, why didn't you go to the monastery? Where were you? I was very worried when they contacted me. We all were."

A version of the truth was always best.

"Some political events prevented me. I was there in Sichuan, but got sidelines."

"But why didn't you just tell them you were delayed? And is it too much to ask that you keep us abreast of your whereabouts? Let us know you've safely arrived in a new country?"

"When you were thirty, did you always tell Grandma your comings and goings? And yes, it would have been better had I told the monastery I'd be joining them a few weeks later. I wish I'd done that. Maybe it was complicated for me because I wasn't doing what His Holiness had instructed me to do."

"Ah. That makes sense. I know that wouldn't sit well with you."

Mom carried her plate to the sink. Her brown hair was still long. She was tall and thin and looked younger than she was, but I noticed some deeper lines in her face, since the last time I'd seen her.

She turned to face me. "Is Jamie okay? Is she why you're here?"

I stared at my mom without answering, thinking of myself days earlier, getting angry at Jamie and telling her it was always painted as my fault when she hurt herself. I realized how untrue that was. I thought again of the track marks she'd cut into her leg that I'd seen as she lay sleeping in her room upstairs in this apartment. My mom always thought I could solve Jamie's problems, not that I caused them. I had promised Jamie that I wouldn't tell our parents what she had done this time.

"Jamie's fine. I'm here because the Dalai Lama asked me to help him arrange his visit. He'll be here in just a few weeks."

"Good. I hope you stay awhile." Mom came back to the table and sat down again. She pressed my hand and then pulled away, with an embarrassed smile. "I'm being like Grandma. I just want to touch my kids and hug you both close."

"Grandma just does it." I squeezed my mom's hand.

"Thanks, David. I have to go see two more clients. But we'll see you tonight, right?" she asked.

"I'll be here. Dinner with you and Dad, seven o'clock."

Mom stroked the side of my head. "Just tell me, is Jamila really okay?"

"Yes, she really is."

"Okay. You and your sister will always have each other."

This implied a deep accomplishment that she'd played her part in, yet I heard a note of sadness in her voice too, for all the people, herself included, who did it alone, without a twin in the world.

BACK IN NEW York indefinitely, I began volunteering in the New York Office of Tibetan Buddhism. My job was arranging domestic flights and ground transportation, overseeing construction of temporary prayer shrines, and taking care of dozens of other logistical details.

In my first week, I brought in two other volunteers who I knew from the New York Buddhist community. Krishna, originally from Woodstock, had been raised in a Buddhist community. She was about five years my junior, and full of optimism and a get-it-done attitude. And there was Jenga, an old friend and practitioner who I'd taken my vows with on my first trip to Dharamsala. He was a gentle, willowy, grey-haired grandfather. He came in each day asking how he could help and set himself to any assignment with the same pleasant disposition.

The days passed quickly as the Dalai Lama's visit rapidly approached. One day the front door opened and there stood Fallon Longo. I jumped out of my chair and rushed toward him but stopped short, not knowing if he would welcome such a demonstrative greeting. But Longo opened his arms wide and we embraced tightly.

"Hey, old friend," Longo said as we moved apart.

"Hey to you!" My voice boomed too loudly and I felt the foolish grin on my face but didn't care. The last I'd heard about him, he was at a monastery in Bhutan and had taken a vow of silence.

"You've ended your vow?"

"Six months ago."

"And you've been in New York?"

He shook his head while looking around the room, elusive as always.

Krishna came toward us with her hand extended. "I don't believe we've met. Krishna."

"Hello. Fallon Longo."

Jenga stepped forward and hugged Longo too. "Hello, old friend. Good to see you."

I grinned like a delighted child.

Longo looked at me with a familiar smirk. "Why don't you put me to work, pip-squeak."

The four of us worked amicably, dividing the days' tasks each morning. Though Longo's vow had ended, he remained mostly silent nonetheless. He communicated with as few words as possible. We all understood instinctually not to ask too many questions. I limited my expectations of our friendship but was still immensely pleased to have him there. Longo was older than me, but that was not the reason he had always seemed three steps ahead of me as a practitioner. He had a recognizable calling, what was commonly known as imprints, the vestiges of enlightenment he'd attained in past lives.

AT THE FIRST Buddhist retreat I attended, a hundred miles outside London, I was an oddity: a ten-year-old boy from America, an observer and helper, not a student. The youngest actual student, a Canadian, was Fallon Longo, who was twenty. Everyone called him Longo. The Dalai Lama and several of the students knew him already, because his parents were Buddhist scholars and students of a great Rinpoche in Toronto. I was nervous around him because the Dalai Lama had asked him to look out for me. Actually, he'd said, "Be his friend," and in Longo's silence I sensed resentment of the assignment.

On our second day in England, we sat on prayer mats in a circle beneath a giant oak tree for the afternoon teaching. The ground was covered in acorns, like beads of polished wood. I chose three and rattled them around in the cup of my hand.

"In the Tibetan tradition, only a lama, upon dying, can direct his consciousness into its next life." The Dalai Lama paused for that to sink in. That morning, I had learned that mere sentient beings cannot direct their reincarnation. Even Tibetan monks can only control their karma to improve the chances of a higher reincarnation.

The Dalai Lama continued. "When I direct my consciousness, as I go out of this world, into its next incarnation, that child will be born a *tulku*—a reincarnated lama—and the child will grow to continue the work of the Dharma."

"He'll be the next Dalai Lama." Longo looked up from the ground, paler even than usual. His obvious discomfort made me think that maybe, like me, he had a fear of saying the wrong thing.

The Dalai Lama drew his robes around his body, looking out over the fields. "I am the manifestation of the Buddha's consciousness." Suddenly raising his arm and pointing down the hill, His Holiness drew our attention to a small gray deer eating acorns under a distant oak tree.

"She will not be the next Dalai Lama. I don't think so. We all strive to not return into the animal realm, because the animals cannot practice the Dharma. But maybe next time for her a human form!" He laughed loudly but then grew serious again. He looked skyward, and his thoughts seemed to float into the tree branches like a group of finches. "Buddha's consciousness is passed through *tulkus* who are temporarily the Dalai Lama, many wicks but the same flame."

There was silence. I looked at the branches of the tree, the sky, the sun patches, and dappled shade in the grassy dirt around us. The Dalai Lama was already like a god in my eyes, and I knew I wasn't alone in my worship of him. Lama means great teacher, and the Dalai Lama was the highest of all.

"Are you a permanent presence on Earth, always here in one form or another?" I spoke before I realized I would. "Like the acorn and the oak tree, life never ends, it just changes forms. The Dalai Lama is always in the world, as the acorn or the tree."

The Dalai Lama stared at me, and I shrank as Longo had earlier. His eyes were twinkling and he exaggerated a shrug—*who knows?* He picked an acorn off the ground and then another, and rolled them in his hand like dice.

His Holiness continued. "Then we are all always in the world. Kundun, one of my many names, too many names, means 'the path.' We are all very important. I hope you will each take the path of the bodhisattva, to lead others out of suffering." He clapped his hands in a burst of energy. "Yes! You can do that."

Each day, after lunch, a varying group of students went for a swim. I always went along with whoever headed down the footpath to the placid green pond, my towel thrown over my shoulder.

One day, in the third and final week, it was only Longo and I going for a swim. We walked together in silence. Dust clouds bloomed from under Longo's sneakers as he stomped along the dirt path in front of me.

Although it was a hot summer day, Longo kept on his long-sleeved shirt. He did a perfect jackknife off the dock, then rose to the surface and swam across the pond with a machine-like athleticism. While I watched from the dock, Longo somersaulted in the water and headed back. As he reached for the dock, I cannonballed into the water and swam out to the middle. Treading water, I watched as Longo did five more laps of the pond. He returned to the wooden dock and did pull-ups from the water. At twenty, he fell backward into the water, and he seemed to rest on the surface. I doggie-paddled closer.

"I can't do that," I said.

Longo swung upright again in the water. "Can't do what?"

"Float."

"You can't float?"

"No, I sink. My legs drag me down."

"Everyone can float—it's holding air in your lungs."

With one kick of his legs, Longo was beside me. He put his hands on my back and raised my body to the surface while he treaded water, seeming as stable as if he were standing. When my body was a flat board on the surface, Longo placed one hand on my abdomen, keeping the other against my back.

"Breathe in deeply and then exhale very slightly. Only breathe from the top ten percent of your lungs. The rest of the air stays in."

I opened my eyes and saw nothing but blue sky. The day of the shooting came rushing at me. Longo's hands on my body felt exactly like those of that other man who had touched me after he knocked me over, right before he was shot and killed. I remembered the man's colors. I had asked His Holiness about the colors when we'd first met, but it wasn't until this moment that

I understood I had seen the dead man's consciousness departing its current form.

"You're doing it," Longo said.

I pressed my chest higher, holding the air inside me, and tensed my stomach muscles to lift my thighs, legs, and feet. The sky was my magnet. I kept my eyes locked on the blue, and my concentration tightened around my breath. Ten percent in and out, my lungs staying full, my muscles pulling upward and upward. *You're okay. You're okay. You're doing it.* I chanted in my head to the young man who had died at my feet, and to myself, who was being born all the time.

Chapter 9

Jamila

I SAT ALONE at my desk at work and stared at the phone. Various lines were lit or flashing. Throughout the building, staff members were talking to girls or making calls on their behalf. I was supposed to be a source of stability to these girls, but my own problems had been taking me from them, starting with my meeting Salam in the bookstore on an ordinary spring day.

Out my window, nothing had changed. In the neighbors' yard, the black mother cat and her two calico kittens jumped through the trash. Cars whizzed down Twentieth Street. Sunshine was everywhere. But summer was finally over. In retrospect, I realized there had been telltale signs that Salam was sick—some weight loss I'd noticed, multiple doctor appointments he mentioned. But most of all, his stare. Salam stared at me in a way that made me think he was memorizing my face, preserving a memory. I assumed I had the same way of looking at him. I'd thought it was love.

I had spoken to Salam from this desk many times. I could still hear his voice saying, "Okay, angel," as a closing to our conversation. I was flooded with memories of us: Salam signing his book to me with that faraway expression, his face when he saw me sitting at his bar, the first time he unpacked baking ingredients in my kitchen, drinking ice coffee with Kahlua on his roof during the July heat wave. These were moments that were stolen outside either of our lives. We'd shared three months of time, withdrawals from each of our lives, to meet in a different world. And that world closed up and vanished, when he pushed me away and I almost killed myself, when Chitra appeared at my house, and when I learned Salam was dying.

I didn't want to act like he was already dead if I didn't have to. Without giving it more thought, I picked up the receiver and dialed Salam's new home number that Chitra had given me.

"Hello," Chitra answered.

"Hi, it's Jamila. I was wondering if I could come by to see Salam again."

"I said you could."

"Okay. Would the weekend be good?"

"That's fine."

"Thank you. Can I bring you anything?"

Chitra paused. "Will David join you again?"

Her question caught me off guard. "I think he might be busy working."

"Either way." She hung up.

I had to smile. Chitra liked David, despite his relation to me, and I was going to see Salam again.

I heard slow footsteps on the stairs. Felicia appeared with a bundle of pink blanket in her arms.

She grinned, her very white teeth like a flash of lightning across her face. "I had the baby."

"Felicia!" Tears sprang to my eyes. "Come here!"

Felicia laughed. "I knew you'd get all excited."

She lowered herself onto the chair next to my desk and laid the baby flat in her lap so I could look at her. The baby's sleeping face was capped by a pink and blue hospital hat. Everything about her was so diminutive and peaceful, her miniature face, and hands like tiny starfish folded under her chin.

I had my first glimpse of the beauty in Felicia's choice. This girl had become a young woman and was now a mother. She deserved attention to the miracle, not merely the mistake.

"She's incredible. When was she born?"

"Almost two weeks ago. On a Sunday. I called you here when the labor got painful, even though I knew the office was closed." She smiled shyly, wanting me to know that she had wanted me at that critical time. For the first time, I imagined being at Felicia's birth, that she might have actually asked me to if I hadn't been so absent recently. But Felicia had gone into labor the same day I had swallowed a bottle of sleeping pills. I was floored by the awful coincidence. I'd failed her. I wasn't there for her in so many more ways than she knew. I wasn't a strong enough person to support Felicia, an eighteen-year-old new mother.

I exhaled. "How did your labor go?"

"It hurt like hell! And the pushing—it's like a melon coming out your butt. But I had two midwives. They reminded me of you. They held my hand and rubbed my back. They cheered for me. I got her out in ten minutes."

I heard the pride in Felicia's voice, and I noticed her eye wasn't wandering as she looked at the baby. I wiped away my tears. "What's her name?"

"Ayana."

"Beautiful. She's amazing, so perfect."

I couldn't take my eyes off the baby. I was reminded of Grandma saying that Melody was perfectly formed, but dead.

"I'm breastfeeding her too, it's healthiest."

I laughed. "I'm so proud of you."

We both stared at Ayana.

"How are you feeling?" I asked Felicia. "Are you managing to get sleep?"

"Yeah, she sleeps all the time. Do you want to hold her?"

"I'd love to."

Felicia shifted the bundled baby into my lap. Ayana sighed and stretched like a kitten.

"Can I have the snack key? I'm hungry. I'll set up snack for group."

"You're here for group?" I teased her.

"You know I don't miss group."

I opened my desk drawer and handed her the plastic key chain, my other arm wrapped around the baby. As she headed for the stairs I said, "Felicia, I'm really happy for you."

Felicia smiled broadly and skipped down the steps.

Looking in to the face of a newborn was like witnessing the future of humanity. Pure possibility. This tiny new person was just starting her time on the planet. Her hundred years might contain anything. All things being what they should, Ayana would live to see a future world I wouldn't know.

I whispered to the sleeping infant, "I want you and your mama to have everything you need."

Felicia returned with an armload of pretzel bags, juice boxes, and mini-muffins.

"I'm gonna eat mine now."

She popped open a bag of pretzels and logged on to the teen computer near my desk. Ayana opened her eyes and looked into my face. She registered no surprise to see me.

"Felicia, are you scared at all?"

She turned slowly from the screen. "Of what?"

"About her being here . . . about being a mother." I looked back to Ayana who was working her lips in the air, expecting a nipple to appear.

"No, I'm not scared. Is that why you don't have kids?"

I looked up at Felicia. There was no judgment in her question. I was just past the age at which I should have had kids, in her eyes. I was thirty.

"Maybe. I don't know my own future. That scares me."

She nodded knowingly. "You'll have a good life, Jamie."

Tears stung my eyes. I was confessing my insecurity to a girl who had so much less security than I did. Could it be she was more experienced in life than I was?

"Thanks, Felicia." I shifted the baby upright so that we were face to face. "I think both of you will too."

"I know." Felicia tossed her wrappers in the trash. "I'm just gonna read my parenting tip for the day." She turned back to the screen.

CHITRA LOOKED DIFFERENT this time when I arrived at their apartment. She wore a short dress over leggings. Her eyes were made up. I didn't know what to make of the effort she'd put into her appearance.

She closed the front door and turned to look at me.

"David couldn't join me."

"No matter." Chitra glanced at the closed bedroom door. I thought maybe it did matter, that in fact she had dressed with him in mind. "Go on in. I think he's awake."

I entered the dark bedroom silently and this time went straight to the bed. I sat beside him.

"Salam."

His eyes opened, and he drew one arm out from under the sheets.

I clasped his hand in both of mine. My head lowered, I heard him softly laughing. When I looked up, I saw the amusement in his shining eyes.

"What are you laughing at?"

"I knew you had guts, Jamila. Showing up here again."

"You have guts. Big, fat, smelly guts."

"Those aren't my guts," he whispered hoarsely. Salam removed his hand from me and pushed himself higher in bed. He tried to smooth his hair.

I stroked the blanket and cupped his knee underneath. I studied his expression. He was content. He was entitled to this conversation and to our affair. He was entitled to his fleeting pleasures because he was dying.

"When did you tell Chitra about us?"

"My blood results changed very suddenly. I don't have much strength now. I told her about you. I suggested maybe you could care for me. But, she got right on a plane."

I was incredulous. "I would have taken care of you—but she's your wife!"

"I know. I was wrong."

I thought of Chitra showing up at my apartment and telling me to leave him alone and my suspicion that she'd helped me, that she'd found me right after I took the pills and interrupted what could have been a successful suicide attempt. Holding Salam's hand, I realized she hadn't told him. Whatever she'd seen, whatever she knew about me, she hadn't told him.

"You could have told me you were ill, you know. Did you think I'd never have to find out?" A tear rolled down my cheek.

Salam pressed his lips together. "I didn't plan on concealing it. But then you loved me and you didn't know I have leukemia, and there was this one beautiful place where it didn't have any impact. I realized how much I needed that, someone to love me who didn't know—pure and simple—without pity or sadness."

"What makes you think I loved you?"

"Jamila. You love me." His face was playful.

"I don't have the guts you think I have," I said.

"You're an angel. Thank you so much for shining on me."

"You're welcome. I did it for the joy of it, you know."

"Even better."

I said goodbye to Salam when it was clear he needed rest.

Chitra looked up when she heard the bedroom door shut, and then turned back to the television and the bowl of ramen she was eating. I approached the back of the couch and looked over her head at the CNN news crawl on the screen.

It was easier to breathe outside of the bedroom, even in Chitra's company. It was unmistakable, his room was a sickroom. The whole apartment lacked light and fresh air. It was stifling in a way it never had been before.

"How do you do it?" I asked.

She looked at me and considered my question. "There's no choice. And I've had two years of getting used to the fact that Salam is sick, and eight months apart from him."

"I really appreciate you letting me see him . . . and say goodbye." My voice broke over the words.

Chitra clicked off the TV and turned toward me, looking and judging, I guessed. But she held her tongue.

"Can I ask you something? Did you come to my place and tell me to stay away from Salam?"

The muscles of her face twitched. "Yes." She glanced at his closed door.

"Was I . . . strange? I mean, did anything happen?"

"You seemed intoxicated."

We stared at each other. Chitra broke eye contact. She unfolded her legs and placed her bowl of soup on the coffee table.

It was time to go.

As I headed for their front door, Chitra said, "You can tell David to call here if he's available to show me around." She shrugged. "He offered to."

"I'll tell him." I hurried out, hiding a smile.

ON WEDNESDAY AFTERNOONS after school, I would ride the bus downtown to West 10th Street, to Anne's office, for my weekly therapy session. The Wednesday before David and I turned thirteen, I stomped into her office, tossed my backpack into a corner of the room, and fell onto the blue-and-yellow-flowered sofa, and slouched low into the cushions.

"Good afternoon, Jamie."

"Good afternoon."

"How was your day at school?"

"Fine. Can I ask you a personal question?"

"You can ask. I may choose not to answer," Anne replied.

Anne had gotten married earlier that year. She wore a thin gold band on her left hand that irked me. For a moment, I contemplated asking her if she was going to have a baby, something I realized I felt threatened by.

"Did you have a bat mitzvah?"

"Yes, I did. In synagogue with two other girls from my Hebrew school class. Not a party, like they do these days. Why do you ask?"

"It doesn't matter."

"Are some of your friends having them now?"

"Some."

"Well, what do you think?"

"I don't care. We don't go to temple, and I never wanted to go to Hebrew school, and then girls are supposed to do it at twelve and boys at thirteen, so what do boy and girl twins do? And besides, David's Buddhist."

"Well, since you're not Buddhist and you're a girl, you could have a bat mitzvah at twelve or thirteen by yourself. If you wanted to."

"It's just a party with really expensive gifts, like you said."

"I'm not sure I said that. It's what it means to the person doing it. Of course, the age of being able to perform *mitzvahs*—good deeds—has traditionally meant becoming an adult."

"I wonder if being a bat mitzvah is like being a bodhisattva."

Anne exhaled a short blast through her nose. Smiling, she said, "You told me bodhisattvas live to serve others. They seek to end the suffering of others."

"Yeah, pretty much." I examined my high-tops, the same basketball style that David wore.

"Hmm. Doing good deeds might be a more down-to-earth version of that. Maybe a successful bodhisattva manages to do it all the time."

I pushed off my sneakers with my feet and folded my legs underneath me.

"Are you feeling like you might be missing something . . . the bat mitzvah?" she asked.

"It's not important. My period was more important."

Anne smiled. "Oh, did you get your period?"

"Yeah, at the beginning of the school year. That's what really makes you a woman. It's not about religion, it's about biology."

"Biology is certainly a big part of our lives, I agree."

"I think humans are animals too."

Anne nodded at me, consenting to humans as animals, and then she waited.

"Do you know what a totem animal is?" I asked her.

Anne nodded again.

"Mine's a wolf. Sometimes I see myself as a wolf, running through the woods. My mouth open, panting and smiling. Sometimes when I'm sick of everyone, David, my parents, even Grandma, I picture myself as this strong female wolf. I raise myself off my haunches and stretch downward and upward, look around, and trot off into the woods, never to come back."

"Does it help? To be the wolf and to run away?"

"It helps a lot. I love that part of myself. I know exactly what I look like, silvery black with yellow eyes."

"It sounds nice, being that wolf."

"The thing that makes me think it might be bad is that the first time I saw myself as the wolf was when I stayed underwater in the pool."

We sat quietly for a few minutes. From the coffee table, Anne picked up a little Guatemalan doll she'd gotten on her honeymoon and touched its hair and blue skirt. Then she put the doll back down and gazed at me.

"Sometimes people just don't make any sense—I don't know what's going on with them at all. But you're not like that, Jamie. You always make sense. You are turning into a young woman. Having a fantasy of being a strong female wolf can be a very healthy thing—what happened in the pool was not. But if you can give yourself strength and independence by being the wolf in your mind, that's a great tool."

I pulled my knees into my chest. I loved it when Anne admired my resilience, my resourcefulness.

The wolf was a comfort and an escape, but I also sensed danger in her presence. When she appeared at the edge of the clearing in my mind, she seemed to beckon me. I wanted to follow her, become her. I yearned to find my own way in the forest, to drink from the stream, sleep in my den, howl at the moon, eventually find a mate and raise my pups.

What I didn't tell Anne was how much it hurt sometimes not being the wolf.

I went into my dad's study that evening while he was writing up notes from the days' clients. He looked up for an instant and then kept writing. A few minutes later, he seemed surprised I was still there. He took off his reading glasses.

"What's up?" he asked.

"Do you believe in God?"

"Oh. I thought you were going to ask me a hard question."

I leaned against his desk. "Do you?"

"I probably never really believed in God. But after Vietnam, I knew I didn't."

"You never talk about Vietnam."

"Not to you, I don't. If I do, it's to other people who were there, or maybe your mother."

"Is that why we don't go to temple for the holidays, because you and Mom are atheists?"

"We don't go to temple because they sell tickets, and Mom and I don't believe in buying tickets to practice Judaism. Would you like to go to temple?"

"No. I've been with Grandma."

"That's right." He looked at me with narrowed eyes.

"But what about having a bat mitzvah?" I asked. "Do you think it matters about becoming an adult and doing good deeds?"

My dad smiled at me, but it was a sad smile. "Jamie, my girl, you have been doing good deeds since the day you learned to talk, since your first steps, you've been angelic."

I looked down, knowing the pain I'd caused him already. I moved to his chair, and he put his arms around me.

He went on. "I don't think there's a special day, or words, or a ceremony that make anyone become an adult. It's incremental, little things along the way that make us more and more grown up. I see you growing up in different ways all the time, and I expect it will continue for years."

I leaned my head on my dad's shoulder, as I'd done when I was that little girl taking first steps.

I WAITED FOR David in front of a cafe. He'd been back at our parents for the past week, and we hadn't seen each other. I was thinking about Chitra—how she was managing to care for Salam in a strange city. I wondered if New York was a hateful place to her, a dirty crowded city, barely seen from within a small, dark apartment where Salam lay ill. She couldn't possibly love New York like Salam did. It represented his illness and his infidelity. So when Chitra approached me on the sidewalk, I thought it was a waking dream. I expected to blink and see another woman who looked remotely like Chitra. But then David was nervously waving to me, and the reality hit. He'd invited her to our lunch date.

The three of us loosely pulled together on the sidewalk.

"We just took a yoga class. I'm starving," David said self-consciously.

He opened the door to the cafe and held his arm out for us to pass. Chitra went in first. As I entered, David mouthed, "Sorry."

We picked at our lunches, mostly with David and Chitra talking about yoga and some of the places she wanted to see in New York if she could get away.

"Jamie," Chitra said in her clipped Mumbai accent. She held out her cupped palm to me, containing the silver key ring I used to possess—the spare set of keys to their apartment. "Would you like to go see Salam now, while I'm out for the afternoon?"

I surmised that David had called Chitra and invited her to a yoga class and then lunch. Were the keys her reciprocal gift? I took them from her and left before my courage escaped me.

My heart hammered as I let myself into Salam's apartment, as I used to before everything had changed. I put my bag and the lunch I'd brought for him on the floor. I moved quietly down the hall, aware that Salam wasn't expecting me, and rapped on the closed bedroom door. There was no reply. I knocked louder and leaned against the door, listening.

"Jamila," Salam breathed in my ear, from behind me.

I swung around terrified. "Oh my God! What are you doing?" I clutched my chest.

He grinned wolfishly. "I was in the bathroom. What are *you* doing? And how did you get in?" He was wearing only pajama bottoms, and his ribs and even sternum protruded through his skin.

His gaunt face inches from mine, I felt weak and elated.

"Chitra gave me keys. I brought you lunch." I scooted around him toward the living room, putting distance between us. "Are you hungry?"

"If you brought me lunch, I'm very hungry."

Salam followed me, not asking for or needing more information.

His kitchen table was covered in the new red tablecloth I'd noticed and imagined Chitra had brought over from home. She'd let me come see him without her being home. She'd sent me. For the first time since I'd learned of Salam's illness, he was on his feet, walking through the apartment with me. The space, and the two of us in it, hung between familiar and foreign.

"Do you want to eat in here?" I asked.

"Yes, like a civilized person . . . I'll go put on some clothes."

Salam seemed to share my anxiety.

We sat at the table. I watched Salam pick at the salmon and lentils I'd brought. It seemed like an effort for him to sit upright and eat. I tried not to stare. He was freshly shaved, but there were patches of stubble along his jaw he had missed. My ears were alert to the front door, anticipating Chitra's early return—a change of heart.

Swallowing, Salam said, "I can't taste very much."

He was being matter-of-fact, without self-pity. I was ready for straight-talk too.

"Salam, have you been given a prognosis? Do you know how much time you have left?"

He nodded. "Weeks to a year. Probably a few months." Now he started to cry. "I'm actually not thinking much about myself. I've had more than two years to accept my illness and the fact that I won't live a long life. I've fulfilled some long-standing dreams this past year—like living in New York. I met you . . . got to know you."

He sat back and ran his hands through his hair, then abruptly folded his hands on the table only to raise them again aimlessly. He rose and put his mostly full plate in the sink.

"Thanks for the food, my love." He turned around and leaned back onto the countertop for support.

"Don't call me that." We locked eyes. "I don't know how to respond to it."

Salam returned to the table and sat. He grew shy, his gaze resting on my crossed arms.

"Falling in love with you was a first for me."

He had never told me he was in love with me. I crept into Salam's lap as gently as I could. I wrapped my arms around him, feeling all his ribs along his back.

"It was for me too."

Salam stroked my hair with one hand, holding me close with the other arm. After a few moments, he said, "Jamie, I have to tell you something."

I sat upright and wiped my nose. "What?"

"You're crushing me. Can we go in the bedroom?"

Salam removed his jeans and climbed into bed, pulling the sheet over his body. He leaned back on the pillows and sighed deeply. I pulled a chair up to his bedside. I felt strengthened by his confession of love, as well as baffled by it. The facts remained the same. He was married. He was dying of cancer. Yet our relationship was progressing in spite of it all.

Salam gazed at the ceiling. He appeared exhausted but also at peace. He could discuss his marriage, and his impending death, and somehow he was still content to be reclining there beside me.

He scooted backwards in bed and patted the mattress. "Come closer."

I looked at the open bedroom door.

He said, "It's okay. Go shut the door and come lie here with me."

I fumbled to take my shoes off and then eased myself under the covers. I pressed my back against his chest, spooning into him. His knees found their place behind mine. I closed my eyes and felt every place where we touched.

"Jamila?"

"Yeah," I whispered.

"I feel shy."

I whimpered, "Me too. This is no good."

He shifted away and stretched onto his back. I stayed curled on the edge of the bed, facing away from him.

"Listen, things have changed between Chitra and me. We're not married in the typical sense, romantically. We want to start letting go while I'm still alive. I know this could be strange for you—you may not want it anymore—but Chitra and I discussed that you and I could be intimate together."

I didn't move a muscle, but felt the same shock run through me as I had when he told me he was married, when Chitra told me he was dying.

Salam raised himself and peered over my shoulder at my face. He didn't try to touch me.

"I'm so sorry, Jamie. I want you so selfishly."

I rolled over and faced him. "There are a thousand reasons I shouldn't be able to make love with you." I stroked his cheek with my thumb and caught his first tears. We kissed. Holding me shakily, he gave me a dozen tiny kisses on my trembling mouth.

I couldn't help responding to his touch, his mouth, his body's scent of baking bread and almonds. He pulled at my clothes. I helped him. When I was naked, Salam took off his boxers and pulled the sheets up over our bodies and heads. I looked at his thinner naked body in the muted light.

I moved toward him and began to cover his chest and stomach and hipbones with tiny kisses. His body arched with pleasure. I committed the silken texture, the yeasty scent, the precise color of his skin to memory.

We made love with many sighs, and sharp cries, and some laughter. We changed positions frequently, trying to make it last as long as possible.

When we were done my limbs were loose and limp and I was filled with gratitude and peace. Salam lowered himself beside me, one arm and leg encircling my body and we slept.

Chapter 10

David

A COUPLE WEEKS before the Dalai Lama was to arrive, Longo tapped me on the shoulder and handed me an email he'd printed out. I watched his rounded shoulders in a threadbare button-up shirt, his shaved head bent toward the floor, as he turned and walked away.

The email was from His Holiness. It read: "New invitation to Rinpoche Chogyam Trungpa's Shambhala Mountain Center—should stay three days there. I want two speaking engagements—University in Boulder. My dear Fallon, is this a good visit for you and David to come?"

I felt my old competitive jealousy of Longo that the Dalai Lama had written to him and not me. Nonetheless, His Holiness was inviting both of us to accompany him to Boulder. I crossed the room to the desk where Longo worked.

"Do you want to go?" I asked, hearing my voice break in a high note.

Longo leaned backward, tilting his chair, his head falling back. He grinned at me. "Diana Mukpo, you know, Trungpa's widow and the Sakyong Wangmo, spiritual queen of his lineage, has a dressage school there too. We could see her horses."

I stared at him in disbelief. Was he impossible to know?

Longo laughed. "Of course we should go. What else would we do?"

"I could go start my studies at Kirti."

Longo dropped all four legs of his chair to the floor. "That's not what you want to do."

"Fine. Tell him yes." I turned away, dismayed by my resistant mood.

"I already did."

I turned back, but Longo was facing his computer again.

The phone on my desk rang. I picked it up on the first ring.

"Guess who wants to get out and about with you?" Jamie said.

"You."

"Not this time. Chitra asked me to give you her number."

"What?"

"Are you in a bad mood?" Jamie asked with amusement. "You sound . . . unusual."

"I don't know. Are you in a good mood? You sound unusual."

"*Ooh*, you are in a mood. Would you take her number? She's been nice to me."

"And what, take her out?"

In truth, I could readily picture exactly how I would take Chitra out somewhere, what I might show her of the city I grew up in. As much as the prospect of traveling with the Dalai Lama and Longo filled me with uncertainty, the prospect of an afternoon out with Chitra was a certain pleasure.

CHITRA AND I waited in the darkened foyer of a yoga studio for the class before ours to end. I studied our bare feet. Chitra's feet were small and the color of tea. The ball, arch, and heel formed elaborate curves. Mine were pale and flat, and my heels had thick calluses from my all-day treks in the hills of Tibet, looking for Lobsang.

We unrolled our mats, side-by-side in the back of the room. Kundahlini breathing emptied my lungs and blood of stale energy. My nostrils exhaled in short forceful bursts, awakening my lungs to their job.

The class began chanting "Om."

The room rang with our synchronized voices, but I easily made out Chitra's voice, worried about what I was doing, spending time alone with Salam's wife. I quickly drew my attention back to the present moment. The repetition of sun salutations calmed me. In warrior pose, my forward thigh felt like an arrow pulled taut in a bow, ready to fly.

When class was over, we went to separate dressing rooms to change back into street clothes. Back out on the sidewalk, Chitra stood before me awkwardly.

"Thanks for inviting me to the class, David."

"Would you like to get something to eat?" I asked, noticing my palms were sweating. "I'm sorry. I should say, I'm meeting Jamie for lunch. Would you like to join us?"

"I guess she never gave *me* any warning." Chitra smiled.

I felt I was playing a fast-moving game to which I knew none of the rules.

As we approached Jamie on the sidewalk, her faraway expression turned to shock. I tried to make eye contact, to tell her with a look that I was sorry. Twin speak. But she turned away from me.

The three of us sat on barstools at a tall table surrounded by sunlight. Chitra and Jamie both picked at their salads. Chitra sipped orange juice through a straw.

After about fifteen minutes, Chitra looked up at Jamie. "Would you like to go see Salam now? I can give you the keys, and I'll come home a bit later."

"I'll get him something to eat from here." Jamie collected her things and raised her hand, waving goodbye to both of us. "Talk to you later," she said to me and walked away. I watched her through the picture window, her head pointing down at the sidewalk, her steps hurried.

Chitra reached into her bag and pulled out a rolled-up piece of brown paper that looked like a cigar. She unfurled it. In purple ink with lovely architectural handwriting, she'd written a list of things to do. She turned the paper to me and held its curved edges down for me to read.

Union Square
Times Square
The Empire State Building
a dog park
Astoria
Coney Island
Central Park
The Statue of Liberty
Harlem- 125th Street
Ground Zero

"I can help you with some of those," I offered with false nonchalance. Showing Chitra around town, spending time alone with any woman, was hardly something I was accustomed to.

She slid the paper back, read it quickly, and let it roll back up. Jamie used to make such lists when we were young. She would fill her backpack with supplies—a subway map, snacks, her wallet, and other incidentals—and head off, sometimes with me and sometimes alone, to roam around the city, crossing things off the list.

"Do you meditate every day?"

"Ha! Yes, among other things."

"Like what?"

"I'm working at the Office of Tibetan Buddhism right now, organizing a tour for the Dalai Lama. He's coming to the States in a few days."

"You'll travel with him?"

"Actually, I will."

I realized with embarrassment that I was trying to impress Chitra.

"You know, I don't live here, in New York, I'm just visiting Jamie and then this work came up."

"So where do you live?"

"Most recently, Dharamsala. Right before coming here I was in Tibet though. I'd intended to study with a teacher there. I'm not really sure what will come next."

"So, we live in the same country." Chitra placed her fork and knife across her plate and laid her napkin over it. I imagined she was contemplating her own return to India, and what that meant about Salam.

"What's your life like in Mumbai?"

"I don't know. Like you, I was doing one thing, and when I go back I'll be doing another."

"Would you like to take a walk to Washington Square Park? There's a dog park. I noticed that's on your list."

Two hours later, when we returned to Soho and Chitra's block, she hardly seemed to notice where we were.

"When my grandma became senile," Chitra said, "she was constantly seeing and talking to ghosts, her dead relatives. One day, my father knocked on her front door and she thought he was her own deceased father. She cried out with joy, '*Yi! Papa!*' She took him in her arms, weeping tears of happiness. She knew he was dead though, and she loaded him down with fruits and flowers, and even scribbled letters to bring to her other relatives in heaven. My father came home with all her offerings, and we ate the spoiling fruits."

It was amusing to imagine Chitra and her siblings gobbling up their grandma's heavenly fruit basket.

"I feel homesick now." Chitra looked up, seeing her own temporary apartment building in a foreign city, with her dying husband inside it. "Oh, we're here already."

She sighed, and I felt it was done in confidence. "Thank you, David, for the lovely afternoon."

"I had a great time."

Our afternoon had felt exactly how I had imagined a perfect first date would feel. I had never really been on one, and I certainly shouldn't have been feeling like a few hours with Salam's wife was the best date I'd ever been on—but I did.

"We should do it again—a museum or something." I was winging it, inexperienced, unpracticed and full of new desire.

"Okay . . . probably. I'll be in touch, okay?"

"Sure. I understand."

Because she'd given Jamie her keys, she rang her own doorbell and waited to be buzzed in. We both looked up at the building.

At the sound of the buzzer, Chitra pushed open the door. "Thanks again. Bye." She disappeared.

Jamie exited the building a few minutes later. "You're unbelievable."

"I'm bumbling along. How do normal people behave?"

"They tell their sister when they're bringing her ex-lover's wife to lunch. Let's get away from their building." Jamie pushed me along the sidewalk. "You're so green."

"I'm sorry, Jamie. It was like I wasn't in control. I invited her to a yoga class, and then before I knew it, to lunch."

"You're lucky it worked out the way it did."

"How did it work out?"

Jamie stopped walking. She was smiling and loose, an old Jamie I'd seen less and less of as we'd grown up. She flipped my hair with one hand. "What's going on here?"

I pulled a piece of hair down over my forehead, it reached my chin. "I know. Do you still do haircuts?"

"I do."

"Let's shave it off. Can I come home with you now?"

In Dharamsala, I kept my head shaved like the Dalai Lama and the monks did. It was the simplest choice. Maybe I was anticipating seeing His Holiness. But I couldn't help wondering if Chitra would like me with a shaved head.

In Jamie's apartment, I stripped off my shirt and sat on a kitchen chair with a towel wrapped around my shoulders. Jamie fetched her clippers from the bathroom and sat me by the window, where the fading sunlight was best. She placed her hand on my head and tilted it to the side, raking her fingers upward through my hair, getting a feel for the length.

Her touch made me sleepy and calm. I shut my eyes. Jamie's hand left my head, and there was silence. And then she was crying.

My eyes jerked open. Jamie held the clipper in one hand, with the other hand resting over the shaver's teeth. Her chin was on her chest as she stood there wailing like a little child. I rose, letting the towel fall to the floor.

"Jamie, what is it?"

"It's got his hair in it." She sobbed. "I cut Salam's hair last." Her fingers caressed the short plastic blades. "David, he's going to die. I'll have to let him go."

I smoothed Jamie's back as she wept in my arms. It suddenly seemed to me that Jamie was a person who always had to let go. We all were, but some were tested more than others. I couldn't think of a single great loss of my own. Perhaps the greatest loss I'd ever witnessed was in that room of Tibetans, haggard from their journey to meet their beloved leader. His Holiness' child-like grief to meet his countrymen and say goodbye forever in the same moment. His loss of country. The sound I'd heard over the phone—the Dalai Lama's breath like something torn apart because he couldn't hold and comfort his brothers as they burned to death in Tibet.

Jamie pulled away from me, but held firm my shoulders. "You're here now, David, like when we were kids, holding hands, thinking the same thoughts. But you'll be gone again soon. You have your Dharma, all that enlightenment ten feet above the Earth. But all I ever wanted was the thing I'd always known . . . us.

"And now I've found it again with Salam. But I can't have him." She searched my face for some understanding. "Don't you ever feel abandoned, David?"

I stared at my twin. No words came. My mind's eye was carried to the dusty roads of Sichuan, my endless footsteps in pursuit of Lobsang. The deep and insatiable desire to connect with him that overtook all other actions.

Ever able to read my mind, Jamie said, "What happened to you in Tibet, David?"

"I met a survivor, a self-immolator. I'd heard of him two years ago, when it happened. He was a monk at the same monastery I was supposed to attend. His name is Lobsang. When I saw him, I became totally obsessed. I searched for him for weeks. I stalked him. When I finally got to speak with him he wanted nothing to do with me."

"What did he want?"

Her question startled me. It was a question I hadn't asked.

"I guess he wanted to get out. But I got out instead. The very same day I spoke with him I called you and I bought a plane ticket to get out of Tibet."

"The morning I was leaving Sichuan another man self-immolated. I was there with all the villagers; we witnessed it. We'd all run to see what was happening. A rumor must have spread, but I didn't understand what people were saying. A man suddenly appeared in the square on fire and then the Chinese police shot him."

Jamie let go of me and pressed her fingers over her eyes. "You should tell Dad."

"Why?"

"He saw a self-immolator in Vietnam. He almost went AWOL."

"He never told me that."

"Ask him."

Looking at her clear and thoughtful eyes, I realized how I'd lived my whole life with another human being who understood me, or at least always tried to. But she had not.

"Jamie, I never feel alone because of you. But I guess you have felt alone . . . because of me."

Jamie's eyes shone like wet stones, and her mouth held the faintest, queerest smile. We reached for each other's hands.

Before I left Jamie's apartment that night, my eyes fell on the clippers on the table. We hadn't used them. They would hold Salam's hairs forever.

THREE HOURS INTO our road trip my father asked, "How do you help people who are in deep pain? How does a bodhisattva do that?" He was driving me back to forestry school in the Monongahela forest, to finish my freshman year. I'd been home for three weeks while Jamie recovered from her breakdown, and we were both returning to our separate schools to complete our first year and finals.

I looked up from my crossword puzzle. Dad had both hands on the steering wheel. His eyes were focused straight ahead on the open highway.

"A bodhisattva's vow is to bring not only himself out of the waters of samsara, out of suffering, but all other sentient beings, as best he can."

Dad's eyes flicked between all three mirrors before he spoke again.

"How did you help Jamie these past few weeks? To make her get up again, stop cutting, go back to school?"

I thought about what Jamie and I had actually done over the past three weeks. The same things we'd done as kids. We ate together, watched TV, took walks, played cards.

"I'm what is called a boatman bodhisattva. I steer the boat with others and myself in it. We leave the waters of samsara together."

"When I first got to Vietnam, I couldn't accept that I had no ability to protect my men. I couldn't spare them from any of the horrors. I was their captain, but had nothing more to offer than they did. I killed myself trying to keep all those soldiers safe, each head, one I needed to keep covered. But I failed anyway. More than once, I lead my men directly to their deaths."

My father stopped talking and drove without taking his eyes off the road. He took deep breaths and seemed to be far away. Eventually he placed his right hand on top of my hand.

"When I came home I became a therapist, wanting to guide and to heal people. To steer the boat, as you say."

This was the most my father had ever spoken to me about Vietnam. I had thought he didn't speak to any of us: my mom, Jamie, or me about his years there. But apparently, he did tell Jamie more.

He continued, "But your mother and I never seem to be able to pull Jamie out of the holes she falls in. Not for lack of trying."

I had an image of myself oaring a wildly swerving raft through churning waters, Jamie peering over the side.

THE DALAI LAMA'S arrival was just two days away. There was plenty of work I could have been doing: press releases to write, arranging each leg of ground transportation with security, the various dietary needs of the Dalai Lama's traveling companions, medical care if it were needed. But instead, I was helplessly lost in the media coverage of Tibet, reading the International section of the Times on-line. Two more self-immolations had occurred, and one of them was a monk. The news in the region and throughout China was all about this new and incongruous trend, Buddhists, even monks, committing suicide.

I read the paper, searching for something that would help make real what I'd seen in the square the day I left. And most of all, hungering for a glimpse of Lobsang, any thread to connect us. Twice I'd seen Lobsang's photograph on CNN, the first holy man to self-immolate, now in hiding since the Chinese authorities had made self-immolation a crime.

The more I read the more I chased away my calm abiding. My thoughts quickly converted to over-stimulated anxiety.

Suddenly Longo was standing behind my chair, looking at my computer screen.

"There's a lot to do here. We're down to the wire and every time I look at you you're searching the internet for self-immolators."

"I am?" I was stunned at having been observed doing this.

Our four desks faced the four directions. In slow motion, Krishna and Jenga turned to look at Longo and then at me. Krishna looked nervous.

Longo put his hand on my shoulder. "Let's take a walk, brother."

Outside, walking along Bowery, Longo warned me, "Pull yourself together. We're all here in New York, in this office working for the same reason and it's what's happening in Tibet, those self-immolators. They're the whole reason we're here."

I rubbed my face with both hands, shielding my eyes with my fingertips. Was Longo right, and I hadn't quite realized what drew us all together now?

"I was just there, Longo. I saw a self-immolator, watched him die. And I met a survivor and basically *harassed* him with my good intentions. I came back to New York because my twin sister tried to kill herself. I was obsessed with this survivor, Lobsang, following him around Sichuan and meanwhile my own twin tried to kill herself here in New York."

"I'm really sorry, David. Was it the first time?"

His question startled me. I shook my head. "The first was when she tried to drown herself. She jumped off a roof once. In college, she had a breakdown; she made cut marks up her leg, like lines on a ruler."

"I was a cutter too."

"You? I tried to reconcile this information with the Longo I'd always known, his advanced Buddhist practice, his calm-abiding.

"Remember in England, when we swam in the lake together?"

"Of course."

"I wore long sleeve shirts, even when swimming, to hide the cut marks on my arms and torso."

"I can't believe it."

"Why?"

"You're a bodhisattva, a Buddhist."

He smiled. "Like those self-immolators? I was there too, David. You met Lobsang after it happened. What could you possibly do then? I studied with him beforehand. I knew what he was planning, and still I couldn't stop him."

"You knew Lobsang?" I asked with quickened breaths. "You were at Kirti? Does His Holiness know this?"

"What doesn't he know? Maybe you were sent to Kirti to clean up my mistakes." Longo tried to say this jokingly but it fell flat.

"There's pain, David. People feel a lot of pain. Your heart is light. You're full of curiosity and hunger. I wondered about your flip side, the reverse of your yang—your twin it turns out. It sounds like she's more one of me."

Longo put his arm around my shoulders and steered me back toward our building.

I thought of the young monks I'd watched play soccer on the grass at Namgyal Monastery. I thought of His Holiness, always with a ready laugh, a twinkle in his eyes. They lived in Dharma wisdom while their Tibetan brothers suffered right across the Himalayan ridge. It was nothing new, to practice Dharma in a world of turmoil. It was the purpose. Longo and Lobsang, and maybe Jamie too, held these contradictions within one person.

CHITRA MET ME in Union Square for our second outing together. I joined a crowd surrounding a group of break-dancers. One spun on his back, placed his neck to the ground, and walked on his hands in tight circles, legs torqued at right angles to the sky.

I saw Chitra approaching from the subway entrance. She was wearing a navy-blue ski cap tugged over her ears. She arrived by my side and squeezed my arm by way of a greeting. Her fingertips poked out of fingerless mittens. In the month since I'd arrived in New York, the season had changed from summer to autumn.

"Have you seen Gandhi?" I asked.

"Not recently."

I took hold of her shoulder, turned her about-face, and led her a hundred paces to the tucked-away garden. A life-sized sculpture of Gandhi walked barefoot in a strip of grass, partially hidden by a young dogwood tree and shrubs. He was wrapped in a *dhoti* and held a walking stick in his right hand. His bronze legs showed the sinews and bones of a determined hero. Someone had pushed a sunflower through his curled bronze fingers. It pointed in our direction.

"I want to touch him," Chitra said.

We stepped over the chain railing and walked up to Gandhi. Chitra stroked one eyebrow of his sculpted face with her thumb.

"America surprises me in these ways." She gestured with a wave of her arm at the entire scene, the statue, the little fenced-in garden, the hundreds of people crossing the square or clustered in groups watching street performers.

We stepped out of Gandhi's garden and walked across the square to catch the 4 or 5 train, but before we reached the entrance Chitra stopped in front of a bench in the sun.

"Can we sit for a minute?"

Chitra lifted her hat off her head, mussed her hair, and pushed it behind her ears. Staring straight ahead, with her hat in her lap, she looked childlike and vulnerable in contrast to her usual elegance.

"Salam is actually doing a little better," Chitra said. "I think it's because he's seeing Jamie and he's happy. I'm convinced he's getting weeks of extended life."

"I should tell you, I don't know anything. It might be better that way."

Chitra ignored me. "Salam and I were never that . . . never in love. Our relationship was always bound up in making plans. First, planning a wedding, as strangers, reporting to each other on arrangements. Then we were separately searching for an apartment. I looked around Mumbai with my mother. He looked on his own. We told each other to check out the places we'd liked.

Weird, but we didn't want to do these things together—we didn't know each other. And then it was culinary school . . . his diagnosis . . . then coming to America."

In some inexplicable way, I wished the conversation was about us and not about them. But I was also exhilarated that she could talk to me.

Chitra pulled her hat back on and stood up. "Let's go to the museum."

In the circular lobby of the Guggenheim, we stood gazing upward into the funnel shaped space. We agreed we'd briskly walk up the entire spiral ramp without looking at a single piece of art and then view each picture on the way down. We climbed, turning our heads away from the paintings, suppressing our laughter. We meandered back down, looking closely at each piece. In my memory, we never once touched hands or elbows or shoulders, even accidentally, but I felt waves of energy between us as she stood by my side, inches away.

Standing on the sidewalk afterwards, saying goodbyes felt impossibly awkward after what had once again felt like a date with another man's wife.

"Nice to see you again," I said, stepping backward, suddenly scared to end up in a hug. But then we just stood and faced each other, four feet apart, without smiling or walking away.

Something told me she was thinking the same thing I was thinking. I closed the gap between us and then we looked at each other from mere inches apart. I reached out and pushed her hair behind her ear, as I'd watched her do numerous times. To my astonishment, she stroked my hair above my ear with a touch so light I barely felt it. I experienced the museum behind us and the surrounding buildings slant to one side. I understood the word swooning.

I kissed her. I kissed her thinking *I'm going to die right after this, and its fine.* Death for this kiss. With my eyes shut, my hands cupped her face. I held her sweet face as we kissed.

Then she pulled away. "I can't do this. I thought I could. Salam is still alive." She looked at me sadly and tried to smile but grimaced. "Sorry, David. I better go."

I was horrified. "Chitra, wait—I'm sorry!"

"I gotta go."

Chapter 11

Jamila

SALAM, CHITRA, AND I sat in their living room, eating bowls of chocolate sorbet with profiteroles they'd baked together that morning. I'd been coming over for the past few Saturdays. Chitra was always out when I arrived, and I would leave before she returned. Salam told me she was exploring the city.

But on that day, she had returned early. It was surprisingly okay to sit, all three of us, eating dessert and watching the news.

And then I blurted out an awkward invitation to my grandma's ninetieth birthday. "It'll be just us, my parents, Grandma, David, and me. We'd love to have you." Chitra let her spoon rest on her chin. Salam looked to her for an answer. I waited.

Chitra stared back at Salam. "Yes, let's go."

MY PARENTS' APARTMENT was open as usual.

"Hello!" I called out, entering the apartment with bouquets of tulips and lilacs and a chocolate birthday cake.

"In the kitchen!" My dad's voice rang out from down the hall.

My mood was buoyant at the prospect of seeing Salam with my family, introducing Salam to Grandma. I put the cake in the fridge, the flowers on the counter beside the stove, and lifted a pot lid to see what my dad was making.

"What can I do to help?"

"Here, peel these." Mom handed me a colander of washed carrots. "You look happy."

"I am." I was feeling new depths of gratitude, brought on by events that my parents knew little to nothing about: I had survived my suicide attempt, I'd banished the wolf for the time being, David was in New York for the longest stretch of time since we were kids living in this apartment, and even the arrival of Felicia's baby girl, but most of all, gratitude for Salam and for all the borrowed hours. I owed a debt to Chitra for allowing me to be close to Salam, to be there for what remained.

As though he were reading my mind, my dad asked, "So you have friends coming? Mom says we're seven."

"Yes, Salam and Chitra."

Dad sliced potatoes into wedges and dumped the pieces into a bowl. "Sounds more like friends of David's."

"What? Oh, yeah. They're from Mumbai. Salam is working here; he's a pastry chef and he wrote a book . . . they both live here now." I was struck by how I couldn't casually explain Salam and Chitra. How was I expecting to share a family meal with them?

"So, Jamie, how's your brother?" Mom asked.

I looked up from peeling the carrots, surprised. "What do you mean?"

"He's barely spoken to us. He leaves early every morning to do his work for His Holiness. And there's the fact that he left Tibet. We don't know why."

I'd been fixated on my secrets. I hadn't thought about how David's arrival home and his not showing up at the monastery in Kirti were unexplained to Mom and Dad. Of course they were wondering, and he wasn't talking. I knew that he'd come home because of me. But I also knew that things in Tibet had gone wrong. My parents didn't know about any of it.

"I suggest you just ask him." I recognized something inverse happening and I couldn't help but smile. "So this must be what it's like to be David. Always being asked, 'How's Jamie?'"

My mom smiled. "Just wait until you're a mother. If it seems to you we worry more about you, you're off on that one, my child. Parents worry. Period."

"I believe you already." I opened a cupboard, looking for vases for my flower arrangements.

DAVID, GRANDMA, AND I sat on the couch, ready for her party to begin. David wore dark gray slacks that I thought I recognized from high school. Looking at his slicked-back hair, I remembered that I hadn't given him a haircut because of finding Salam's hair in my clippers.

I consciously lowered my shoulders. David had been quiet since he'd arrived directly from work at the Office of Tibetan Buddhism. There was no twin-omniscience happening between us; I didn't know how he felt about our special guests, didn't know what he would think upon finally meeting Salam. My heart thrummed with nerves as I wondered why I'd orchestrated this bringing together of all the most important people in my life, who did not belong together.

The doorbell rang making me jump. "I'll get it."

Salam appeared like a vision of his earlier, healthier self, in a button-up shirt and black slacks, with his square-toed leather shoes—his old work attire. He looked like the man I had been dating over the summer, more than the gaunt patient in pajamas he'd become in the last month. He was holding two shopping bags full of their dessert fixings.

But it was Chitra who I couldn't take my eyes off. She wore a cantaloupe-colored sari with delicately bejeweled edges. A glimmering stone was pasted to her forehead, and dark kohl lined her eyes. She was breathtaking. The two of them standing in my parents' open doorway were a dizzying sight.

"I hope I'm not overdressed. I wear these for special occasions at home," Chitra said.

"It's beautiful. Come in."

David helped Grandma stand up from the couch. Grandma peered at Chitra and clapped her hands appreciatively as though she had been hoping a guest resembling a bird of paradise would appear and her wish had been granted. David appeared frozen, he stared at Salam and Chitra with an expressionless face. I knew

Salam's magnetism to be as strong as Chitra's. I could see Salam through David's eyes, and remembered the first time I'd laid eyes on him, almost intimidated by his beauty.

"Grandma, these are my friends, Salam and Chitra. This is our grandma, Lill, the birthday girl."

Grandma shook Salam's hand, bowing her head toward him. "It's so good to meet you." Then she clasped both of Chitra's arms. "I love your outfit, dear—it's beautiful. Come, sit here next to me."

"And Salam, this is David."

Salam held his hand out to David. "I've heard a lot about you. It's a pleasure to finally meet you."

"It's good to meet you too," David stuttered.

At the table Grandma leaned over me toward Salam. "Isn't it a feast? My daughter makes a beautiful table. And all these beautiful ladies to dine with."

"Yes, all the food is delicious and the ladies are beautiful." Salam rested his hand briefly over Grandma's clawed fingers.

I remembered the quickening sensation I felt the first time his hand touched mine. It struck me—*Grandma has met Salam now.* Months earlier, I had fantasized about Grandma meeting Salam because he and I were engaged. That was before I knew he was married, before I took the sleeping pills, and before I learned Salam was dying. Instead, she was meeting Salam as Chitra's husband. I had introduced him as a friend and would never be able to share with her the great person he was to me, or fulfill the dream of her embracing him as my future husband. I had a horrible flash forward to months in the future, saying to Grandma, "Remember that Indian man I brought to your birthday? He died."

Salam shut his eyes briefly, a long blink of exhaustion.

"How are you feeling?" I whispered to him.

He jumped a little. "I'm digging deep." I knew he meant pushing to keep his energy up.

After dinner, I carried plates to the kitchen and helped Mom load the dishwasher. My father made coffee. I covered Grandma's cake with an entire package of birthday candles. Salam and Chitra laid pastry puffs on a platter my mom gave them.

From the fridge Salam took a Tupperware container filled with mango lassi mousse and ladled the fluffy cream into a frosting cone he'd brought. He swirled mousse topping into each pastry. The last puff finished off the mousse, the measurements perfect. It was one of the desserts I had tried that first night in his restaurant, when he'd ordered them all for me. Salam and I were huddled close together over the tray. He pressed out a last dollop of cream onto his finger and made to place the finger in his mouth, but abruptly reached toward me and wiped the cream onto my neck. With a quick look over his shoulder, at the others, he leaned in and kissed the mousse off my throat, grabbing some skin in his teeth.

I touched my neck and swallowed a yelp, as Salam faced the sink and rinsed out the white bag of the icing cone, turned it inside out, and placed it on our drying rack. He wiped his hands and looked at me.

"Can you show me where the bathroom is, Jamila?"

In the hallway, we passed a series of framed photographs of David and me as children, sitting back-to-back, smiling for the camera. Salam didn't seem to notice them and I imagined that Chitra was probably the more observant one, that she was taking in details Salam missed.

"Right here," I pointed, "and no, I will not accompany you in there."

"I'd probably drop dead in your parents' house anyway." Salam stroked my cheek with his thumb. "I'm having a very nice time though." He went in and shut the door behind him.

When I returned to the kitchen, my dad and Chitra had their heads bent over the I Ching, discussing how they both liked to throw their fortunes.

Chitra looked up at me. "Can you show me somewhere I can change out of my sari into more comfortable clothes?"

"You can use my old bedroom." I led Chitra up the staircase and down the hallway. As we walked by David's childhood room, I heard David and Grandma talking quietly in there.

I showed Chitra to my room and started to leave, shutting the door for her.

"Stay a moment please."

She sat down on the edge of the bed and pulled jeans and a shirt from her bag.

"I said okay to this. I gave Salam permission. He should have whatever pleasure he can now. I'd like to see his life end with happiness." Chitra spoke quietly as she pulled off the outer layer of the sari.

She looked at me and gently added, "We're both going to lose him. Don't lose sight of that. This one night out will cost him two in bed."

She stood and stepped toward me and scratched my collarbone with one fingernail. "There's mango lassi on your neck."

My face burned, and I rubbed the spot away.

"Our lives will continue; we'll have more. He won't. This is it. Enjoy the time, and the desserts, as much as he does. But prepare yourself."

"I'll try."

She turned her back to me to begin changing, and I left the room.

Chitra came down five minutes later wearing jeans and a T-shirt, having pulled her long hair up in a ponytail. She was now a different kind of beautiful.

Mom said, "Where's David and Lill? We're ready for dessert."

Chitra did an about-face and sang out, "I'll get them."

I went to the kitchen and lit the candles on the cake. *One flame, many wicks.*

When I heard them settling again at the table, I slow waltzed into the room, the cake with countless fires glowing brightly in my hands.

Salam looked at me with that purposeful look that made me think of memorization. *Please*, I recalled his inscription in my book.

I stood in front of Grandma and lowered the cake where she could see it fully. The room was singing to her. Ninety-year-old eyes reflected each miniature fire, and the granddaughter she'd sent forth into the future was reflected in her eyes too. I watched her make a wish.

TIME SEQUENCE ONE
MONTHS 1-4
SHOCK
THE EARLIEST FEELINGS OF MOURNING INCLUDE THE INITIAL SHOCK (*THIS CAN'T BE HAPPENING*), DENIAL, FEELING OVERWHELMED, AND NUMBNESS.
WHAT DOES THE EMOTIONAL PAIN I WAKE TO EACH MORNING FEEL LIKE?

I put the sheets of paper down on the bed. "What is this?"

"Exercises for preparing to lose a loved one. My doctor gave them to me."

"For spouses."

"That doesn't matter. And I gave them to Chitra too. You don't have to show me what you write if you don't want to. It'll help you when the time comes."

"I don't think I can do this."

I sat up in his bed and folded my legs and took another look at the worksheets Salam had handed me almost immediately after making love. I read aloud.

WHAT DO I DO TO COPE WITH THIS PAIN?
I SEEM TO BE RUNNING ALL THE TIME. IF I WASN'T
RUNNING, WHAT WOULD I BE DOING AND HOW
MIGHT I FEEL?

My wolf was exactly that feeling—an overpowering impulse to be running. Suddenly, I felt I could tell Salam about me. I had the courage to tell him, the inner strength to utter the words. But I didn't need to. I was in some critical way stronger, strong enough to share this terrible thing with Salam, and in fact, strong enough not to tell him. Salam didn't need to carry any additional burdens out of this world. He was working on putting his burdens down.

I touched his face. "If I wasn't running I'd be right here with you. This bed, this room, our little world."

Salam raised the covers, inviting me back in. "Run over here."

THE MONTH AND a half since David had arrived had been the longest stretch of time he'd spent in New York, and the longest amount of time we'd spent together since high school. He was in my daily life in the way a twin craves and hungers for. The Dalai Lama was arriving any day. David would be busy attending to him day and night. And when that ended, I figured David would go home with the Dalai Lama to Dharamsala, or maybe he would return to Tibet, to finish what he started there. Whatever his future held, I was unprepared for him to leave again.

I had a dream about the Dalai Lama. He strode along a dark river alone, a walking stick held firmly in one hand. Stepping out of a dense thicket of trees into a clearing, the Dalai Lama looked in both directions, finding his bearings. He spoke aloud to himself. "I don't know where I'm going." The dream was in black and white, without color it was permeated with sadness.

I woke up feeling I'd shared a private moment with the Dalai Lama. I lay awake in bed. I used to keep a photo of him hidden in my desk as a kid. I'd researched his life at the library, in secret, trying to know a little piece of what David was experiencing.

In the dream I longed to help the Dalai Lama. The thicket and the clearing were nondescript, without landmarks, and I had an aching feeling that he had lost his bearings, that he had no idea how to go forward.

David had once described to me the Tibetans who made the arduous and risky journey, leaving Tibet to trek a hundred miles through the mountains to Dharamsala to meet their spiritual leader, the Dalai Lama. Some stayed in India for months, enrolling their children in the Tibetan school to learn the language, religion, and culture that they were denied in Tibet. Others waited days or weeks for a meeting with the Dalai Lama and then, satisfied, made their way back home across the Himalayas. Everything they needed in life was satisfied by meeting the Dalai Lama. David said that in the days following these meetings the Dalai Lama carried a split heart, half of him travelling home with his countrymen.

"SOMETHING HAPPENED. MAYBE you've heard?"

"What?" I asked, turning to glance at my brother's face. We were walking in Central Park, looking for the changing colors of autumn, the day before the Dalai Lama was arriving.

David stopped suddenly and covered his face with his hands. "I think I hurt someone who's vulnerable. I made a mistake—can we sit down?"

My brother's cheeks were flushed and his eyes were wide and panicky. He looked as out of his element as the day he arrived in New York.

"Why would you hurt someone? You of all people."

"Please just sit." David collapsed on a bench. I sat next to him and peered into his face.

"Does this have to do with Chitra?"

David looked at me with the helplessness of a child, or one of my teens at work, hoping I'd just know what they needed or what had happened to them, that they wouldn't have to say.

"Why do you ask about her?"

"I thought I noticed something at Grandma's birthday."

David covered his face with his arm, hiding.

"What's wrong?"

He took a deep breath and pressed his fingertips into his scalp. "I kissed her."

"Chitra? What the—?"

"I lost control of myself. I feel awful about it. It was kind of mutual, but then she clearly regretted it and ran off."

"I don't understand. When? At the birthday party?"

"No, the week before."

"And then you two sat through that dinner . . . she can't be too upset about it, or she wouldn't have come." I looked at my brother. It suddenly seemed funny and not particularly weird that he and Chitra would like each other. Our connection was like a double flame. A well-matched square.

"So you're not mad at me?"

"Mad about a kiss? I'm not the Grinch. We're sleeping together again, Salam and I. Chitra gave us her permission."

"I figured. She alluded to it," David said grimly.

"Grandma's party was the strongest Salam had felt for many weeks. He's barely gotten out of bed since." I began to cry. "David, he might only have a month to live."

Slowly, David rose to his feet and held out his hands to pull me up. "We should all live life." We headed down the path again.

"David," I linked my arm through his, "do you think I could meet the Dalai Lama?"

Chapter 12

David

I WAS UP early the day of the Dalai Lama's arrival. There were final preparations to attend to in the apartment where he was staying, where I'd be waiting to welcome him and his party. His Holiness and I had communicated a handful of times about the many arrangements and logistics. But we'd had no further conversations about my time in Tibet, my failure to meet the teacher he had selected for me. It was rare to get any time alone with him, but I knew he'd find his moment. I had broken one of the primary commitments of a bodhisattva, of any Buddhist practitioner, to seek and to have a teacher. The epidemic of self-immolations and the ever-tightening repression of the Chinese authorities were of utmost concern to His Holiness, but he would get around to my transgression. Of that I was sure.

There was a knock on my bedroom door early that morning. My dad poked his head into the room.

"Hey there. You got a moment to talk?"

"I was just getting ready to leave, but okay."

He came in and leaned on my desk. It seemed like he politely refrained from looking at the unmade bed or my clothes strewn about on the floor. "Today's the big day, right?"

"Yes. He lands at two o'clock. Longo is picking them up. I'll meet them at the accommodation."

"You must be excited to see him." My dad smiled at me, nervously perhaps. "Mind if I sit?" He gestured to my desk chair.

"Of course not."

He settled in the chair with an appreciative sigh. I sat on the edge of my bed, facing him. "What's up?"

"We've hardly spoken since you got home."

"I guess I've been really busy getting ready for the Dalai Lama's visit. Sorry."

"It's okay. I just want to ask how you are."

I exhaled fully and took a deep breath to slow down before answering him. "I think I'm good."

"Your mom received that email from the monastery—saying that you hadn't arrived as scheduled. We were concerned, and then the next thing we know, you're here. What happened?"

I'd thought about Lobsang many times a day. His disfigured face and his chosen exile from the monastery rarely left my thoughts. And now, I was puzzling over the fact that Longo knew him prior.

"Jamie said I should talk to you about this. Right after I arrived in Tibet, I met a self-immolator who'd survived. He was a monk at Kirti, the monastery I was supposed to enter."

"It's a trend now in Tibet, catching like fire."

"You're aware of it?" I was surprised by my father's knowledge and his dark humor.

"It's in the news. I've followed news of Tibet since you were a kid, well since you became a Buddhist. That's my stake in it, Son. So what does it mean to you? You met him, you say?"

I scooted back on my bed and leaned against the wall, suddenly exhausted.

"His name is Lobsang. I met him and spoke with him. He's no longer a monk, or even a practitioner. He's in a wheelchair and very disfigured. I thought I could help him."

"Ay, what a terrible shame, and the grief that must have led him to do it. How did you imagine you could help him?"

"I don't know. I had no interest in being there. The Dalai Lama sent me, assigned me a new teacher, but I never wanted to go. As soon as I saw Lobsang, it was like I had a reason to be in Tibet."

"Is he in trouble, politically?"

I looked at my father keenly. "Maybe he wasn't a year ago, but now that there are more people doing it, they've outlawed it. He's a wanted man. I've seen his picture twice on CNN."

"So what did you think you could do for Lobsang?"

"Bring him back to the Dharma, restore his faith." I said, sounding vaguely unsure.

"Is that what he wants?"

"No, but that's my point. He's lost his way."

"You know him that well?"

"It's what I think I have to offer."

My father and I sat in silence for several minutes.

"This is why the Dalai Lama is coming. He wants to stop this horrific trend. The day I left Tibet, I witnessed one. I followed the crowd without knowing what was going on. A self-immolator ran through the square, engulfed in flames. It was completely surreal. Then the military police stormed in, and they shot him. They killed him.

My dad braced his head with his hands, and he winced painfully.

"Jamie said you saw one in Vietnam."

Dad's eyes darkened like a sky about to be taken by storm. I was able to see him as a young man, as he had been then.

"I told Jamie about that when she was hurting herself in college, the cutting. I was scared she was thinking of suicide. I'd seen in Vietnam how pain and hopelessness can lead all a person's actions toward their own death. I only told Jamie half the story. A disclosure that I thought was useful to her.

"My men and I found a tiny village in the jungle. It seemed abandoned. We hid at a distance and surveyed the area through binoculars. Almost immediately after we took cover, a man stumbled out into a clearing. He seemed drunk perhaps and he was weeping. He sat on the ground and crossed his legs. He cried into the sky. And then he must have held a lighter or a match to his clothes, which were already soaked in gasoline. He went up in flames, screaming while he was devoured.

"No one came to his rescue. It seemed like he was a decoy. It was my judgment call, my decision to stay two hundred yards away where we were well camouflaged. I thought the Vietcong was trying to draw us out. I watched him burn to death through my binoculars. We stayed hidden there for eight hours. That burnt corpse lay there the whole eight hours. I felt in my own flesh and bones how he cooled and turned into a dead thing, an object left behind. There were no soldiers laying wait for us. It was an abandoned village, and he was AWOL, a defector. He was all alone. We'll never know if we could have saved him. He thought he died alone, unseen. But we were there. We could have done everything, but we did nothing."

I WAITED FOR the Dalai Lama at an apartment on the Upper East Side that had been loaned to him and his closest traveling companions for the week of his visit. It was a four-bedroom apartment with windows that overlooked Central Park, richly upholstered furniture, and gleaming wood floors. It was immaculately clean and airy, and the fourth or fifth home of a garment district heiress who was a Buddhist practitioner.

I prepared the master bedroom for His Holiness with an altar and meditation cushion. I arranged a tea tray and a fruit platter for the entire party to refresh themselves upon their arrival. I had brought with me the *New York Times, Washington Post,* and *Wall Street Journal,* three of the numerous papers the Dalai Lama liked to read daily. I separated and cut a bushel of fresh lilacs and roses, and made an arrangement for each bedroom and the living room where we'd have tea. While I worked, my heart pounded with anticipation at seeing him. After placing a bouquet beside the bed where the Dalai Lama would sleep, I kneeled on the floor and with arms outstretched bowed forward again and again, quietly reciting the bodhisattva's prayer.

My phone chimed in my pocket. It was a text from Longo.

On the Van Wyck, be there soon.

I sat in the living room, awaiting my dear friend and beloved teacher. It would be easy to say no one could have foreseen the current plight of Tibet, the threat of extinction, the swallowing whole by the Chinese majority, and the rash of self-immolations that was quickly becoming a weekly event. Yet sixty years before it was so, Thubten Gyatso, the thirteenth Dalai Lama, His Holiness's predecessor predicted exactly this. He had lived through two exiles from Tibet as well, during a British and then a Chinese invasion. When he returned to Tibet as political and spiritual ruler, he prophesized a full-scale invasion by China and foresaw that the next Dalai Lama would live permanently in exile and have the responsibility of bringing Tibet out of isolation and into the larger globalized world—or else, he feared, Tibetans would see their land and their way of life disappear. No previous Dalai Lama had been known globally as His Holiness is. And no other Dalai Lama had been exiled from Tibet beginning in his youth and most likely lasting until his death.

His Holiness, the fourteenth Dalai Lama, was the leader of a country he had not set foot in since he was seventeen years-old. He was now faced with ordinary Tibetans and even high monks in his homeland abandoning non-violence and setting themselves on fire. His Holiness has stated that he understands them, but does not support what they're doing. I knew his political stance on self-immolation, but not his feelings. I knew he could not abide what my father had endured, to be two hundred yards away, watching through binoculars, while his brothers and sisters morphed from humans to curls of smoke, unseen now and forever, reborn into samsara.

I heard His Holiness's party in the hallway and rushed to the front door. Ten monks with shaved heads piled out of the elevator, all wearing crimson robes, accompanied by Longo and two other attendants in suit jackets who carried suitcases.

And then he stepped through the elevator doors.

He looked at me with a steady gaze. Since I was a boy, at every meeting we'd had after our first encounter at the 92nd Street Y, the Dalai Lama had greeted me with laughter.

I pressed my hands together and bowed deeply. "Welcome, Your Holiness!" Tears streamed down my cheeks.

He reached me at the threshold of the apartment, gripped my arms, and pressed his forehead to mine.

"I'm sorry." I whispered.

"We'll talk." The Dalai Lama withdrew and entered the apartment.

I carried the high monks' suitcases to their rooms and then waited in the living room while the Dalai Lama and the other monks settled into their rooms. Longo took half of the group to a nearby hotel.

After freshening up, the Dalai Lama padded into the living room in slippered feet. His close-cropped hair was damp, and he wore a new crimson robe. He fell onto the couch, in front of the fruit platter, and patted the seat beside him.

"Come."

I moved next to him.

"David, do you know the Mahayana teaching of the burning home?"

I did know the lesson. I had heard this analogy for bodhisattva-hood from a Mahayana Rinpoche in Dharamsala.

"Yes, Mahayana tradition holds that all sentient beings reside in a burning home. Their house is on fire. And yet no one is aware that the house is in flames all around them. A bodhisattva exists to break the cycle of *samsara* and lead all beings out of the burning house."

My thoughts turned to the fliers of lost firemen Jamila had described seeing after 9/11, lost bodhisattvas who saved our literal houses on fire, who didn't make it out that day.

The Dalai Lama lifted his feet from his slippers and drew himself up so that he was sitting cross-legged on the velvety, sectional couch. He removed his glasses and wiped them with a handkerchief. His eyes were downcast, revealing just a sliver of his brown irises. I knew his vision was very weak without the glasses. His face held a calm repose, without expression, and I saw his age and his exhaustion. He replaced his glasses on his face and peered at me.

"If I am your teacher and I send you to study with a new Rinpoche and you do not appear, *and* I am the Dalai Lama, do you think I will not learn of this? I will remind you of the conditions you were given, which are conducive to a Dharma practice. For one, you were given a teacher. So I assume you were leading someone from a burning home, and thus, you could not meet your teacher. Is that right?"

I looked down at my lap. "No. I was too late for that." My voice and hands shook as I tried to explain myself to His Holiness. "I met Lobsang, the self-immolator you told me about two years ago. I tried to reach him, to get through to him, to bring him back to the Dharma. But he's not interested. I let myself lose my way and my purpose there. I know you'd made arrangements for me, you'd assigned me a new teacher, and I didn't follow through. I'm so sorry."

"Kirti is a very small place. Rinpoche Gayto saw you many mornings come to the monastery gate. He hears that you are going to see Lobsang. I cannot put these two old feet in Tibet," he gripped his bare feet which were folded beneath his knees, "but I do send eyes and ears into Tibet."

"Don't forget that brother Lobsang is a bodhisattva too. Do you follow me?"

I searched His Holiness' face with rising fear. I didn't know what he meant. I shook my head, not bothering to wipe away my fresh tears.

"What do you see when you open your eyes and look around in every direction?" His Holiness turned his head left to right then straight ahead and twisting to look behind. His vision was not taking in the walls of the Manhattan apartment where we sat. He looked out at distant horizons. "Does Lobsang see the same things? He is a bodhisattva too. What does that mean about his sight?"

The Dalai Lama lifted up a small package that was tucked into his robe. He held it out toward me.

"For you."

I took the package from him.

The Dalai Lama turned my shoulders to see the back of my head. I had drawn my hair into a stubby ponytail at the back of my neck. He tugged it lightly. "I should have gotten you a comb for your long locks." Finally, he laughed a hearty laugh I'd known and sought after my whole life.

"I'm sorry, Your Holiness."

He nodded at the unopened gift, looking into my face.

I gently tore off the red tissue paper. Inside was an embroidered box. I opened it and saw it contained a pair of meditation cymbals, three inches in diameter, connected by a thin strip of leather.

The Dalai Lama lifted them out. He struck the cymbals—rapping them against each other without his fingertips touching the metal, so the sound rang out clearly, unhindered. Using the leather strap like reins, he turned the cymbals in various directions, guiding the sound toward the east, west, north, south.

"All directions, David. Listen and look in all directions."

A final deep chime stirred the air with vibrations that rang for several minutes in our ears.

When the vibrations faded, His Holiness twirled the leather on his thick fingers, landing the cymbals in my palms. I cupped them like two eggs and drew them to me and examined the engravings inside the thick metal cups. The cymbals I normally used had the eight good-luck symbols of Tibetan Buddhism engraved on them, and they were also thick and heavy and strung on a leather strap. The new pair was slightly larger and much heavier, made from a different metal, perhaps iron, and engraved with Tibetan script, no images.

"Can you read it?" the Dalai Lama asked, his tone making me realize it was a personal message.

"You had these made for me?"

"Yes."

Then I saw that the first characters included my name, *For David.* "When?"

"When my brother Gayto told me you were like a stray dog at his gate."

He'd had them made while I was in Tibet, his words to a missing bodhisattva son. The gift had been planned before I even knew I would flee Tibet, or come back to New York, before he'd called to say he'd be coming here too. I felt his omnipotence, as though his eyes and ears saw and heard me from any distance and that, without effort, he knew me entirely.

I shook my head. "I can't read it."

"You'll look it up. Or maybe a Tibetan will help you." He burst into laughter and patted my shoulder. He'd had his fill.

Two Rinpoches entered the room and came toward the sofas. I rose and bowed to them. Although I did not know them, they each gripped my head and shoulders in a hug.

I poured tea. The Dalai Lama and the other Rinpoches talked quietly in Tibetan, small talk that I understood, about their journey and the rooms I'd made up for them. They rested with their feet up. Although I noticed the peace they carried with them, I couldn't share in it. I held the cymbals in my hands, tracing the lettering with my thumb, wondering what the message would be.

Chapter 13

Jamila

ON THE DAY of my meeting with the Dalai Lama, I went alone to the office of Tibetan Buddhism in Manhattan. The trees that lined the sidewalks had lost all their leaves, so that it was hard to tell whether they were alive at all. The quiet brownstone street, devoid of color brought back my dream about the Dalai Lama lost in the woods. I looked for landmarks or anything I recognized, as he had. I noticed that most trees had one or two leaves left clinging to a naked branch. Of what caliber were these last leaves, when they had been among thousands? Had there been some knowledge within each leaf, that it would be among the very last?

Monks in crimson or mustard-colored robes stood on the sidewalk outside the building, and more were clustered together in the reception area. I stood frozen in the entryway until a young woman seated behind a desk smiled warmly and beckoned to me.

"Me?"

"Yes." She nodded.

I approached her. "Hi, my name is Jamila."

"I know. Follow me. I'm Krishna."

Her serene smile never left her face as she led me into a sitting room with a low wooden table surrounded by cushions on the floor. There were small teacups laid upside-down on a placemat. Krishna returned a moment later with a pot of tea, a curl of steam rising from its spout. I could smell the dark flower of Jasmine.

"May I pour you some?"

"Yes, thank you," I stammered, suddenly unsure of having asked David to arrange this meeting.

"His Holiness will be in to see you momentarily."

I choked nervously on my first sip of tea.

Krishna laughed. "Oh my god, you're so alike."

"Who?"

"Your brother."

Krishna straightened the cups on the table and the teapot on the cozy. "Relax, he'll be right in." She bowed slightly, her hands pressed together below her chin and she left the room.

Alone, I crossed and uncrossed my legs on the cushion, unsure how to position myself. My heart beat too quickly. I hadn't known it before, but I was scared of the Dalai Lama.

I didn't hear him enter the room, but I looked up to find a curtain of crimson beside me. His Holiness' smiling face and glinting glasses seemed to float above his robe.

I jumped to my feet and found myself just inches away from him. I covered my mouth with one cupped hand, feeling what thousands of people feel when they meet this man, understanding what overcame David. The Dalai Lama's enlightenment was like an electrical force crackling around him, deeply loving and yet not harmless.

"Your Holiness, I'm sorry, I'm going to cry."

He squeezed the tops of my arms with his hands and gently laughed. "Ah, there. So good. So nice to have you here."

I wiped at the tears that wouldn't stop coming.

"Sit." His Holiness gestured to the cushion where I had been sitting. We settled on the pillows. "Your brother has been such a help to me. Thank you for sharing your body-mate with me—with the Dharma."

I looked at him, speechless.

"I met David as a young boy, and I knew he was compelled to leave his home to come and find a teacher." He paused and looked at me, within me it seemed. The Dalai Lama's eyes were more inquisitive than any eyes I'd ever seen. "Sometimes Buddha's shoots sprout in far places." He patted my hand on the table and chuckled. "So, I knew he was a bodhisattva in the making. But I didn't know he was a twin."

"I thank you, Jamila. For the Dharma to call on David meant you needed to let him go. He was torn away from you."

My lungs exhaled a deep breath that I'd been holding in since I was ten years old. That was the heart of it. We'd been severed for him to follow this path.

"You had to practice dying."

"Why do you call it that?" I whispered.

"You lost a half of yourself, just as David lost part of himself that was called to something larger than him. To allow David to be separate from you, you had to practice dying."

The Dalai Lama removed his glasses and looked into my face with his naked eyes.

He continued. "Not unlike me as a child raised in a monastery, very lonely, separated from my family, my village, and even more so now, an exile separated from my homeland and my people. Every day is a form of practice dying. Every day I am finding my way."

I pictured him as he had appeared in my dream in that wintry landscape between the woods and a clearing, lost.

"But listen carefully, Jamila. It should be a spiritual practice, a meditation and preparation for death and letting go—not physical violence against oneself. Never that."

His voice was stern, but his face remained soft and compassionate. So David had told him about me, about how I hurt myself.

I saw the Dalai Lama again as in my dream, and color flooded the picture. This time his walking stick struck out with purpose. He knew where he was going. In remembering, the dream was glimpsed anew. It was me walking in the woods, my steps light and sure.

My voice came out a whisper. "Practice letting go of what we love, these smaller deaths."

The Dalai Lama patted my hand exactly the way Grandma did.

"That's it. The only thing any of us can take with us when we die is the spiritual practice we've accomplished. No other accomplishments cross into the next life with you. I think you already know—one life has many small deaths we cross through. You're a twin. You held David's hands in the womb. You held each other's bodies before you entered this lifetime, the bridge time. Perhaps David was the *tulku* who inherited a challenging gift." The Dalai Lama pointed his finger at me. "But it was Jamila with the open heart—the one who had to give instead of receive."

His hands were lined and thick-knuckled. Laugh lines showed around his eyes even in repose. I was close enough to see the silver stubble around his temples, behind the arms of his glasses.

"I hope some of your tears are of happiness."

I touched my cheeks. My tears hadn't stopped but I'd stopped noticing them.

The Dalai Lama smiled. "Some of us seem to be put here to learn lessons." His eyes focused sharply on me. "I believe I am as you are. To experience loss and respond by giving means you're a very strong person. You are helping me, Jamila, to see something I've been struggling with. I've had many years of life, a very fortunate monk, but now I must consider a big change. I must do what is needed, as you do. I thank you."

I sensed that our meeting had come to an end. Like those Tibetan pilgrims who receive the Dalai Lama's full attention for an hour and then turn back for the journey home, I was sated.

"Thank you, Your Holiness." I was overcome with the desire to hug him, and he saw it.

Laughing, he said, "Come, my child," and he pulled me toward him.

I HELD MY address book open to Anne's phone number in Vermont. I'd been thinking of her since the day I took the pills. It was a mixture of things that prevented me from calling my old therapist: respecting her privacy, pride and embarrassment, and knowing that her profound effect on my life wasn't mutual. I was her patient. The day I met the Dalai Lama, I returned home and found myself concentrating on the human connection between Anne and me, two people who'd shared so much of the same time and space. The place where our lives overlapped was big. I dialed her number.

"Hi, Anne, it's Jamie."

"Jamie! This is amazing. I was thinking about you this morning."

"You were? What were you thinking?"

"Oh, I don't know. Nothing specific."

"Please tell me."

Anne sighed good-naturedly. I pictured her twisting an earring while she listened.

"Alright. Well, my oldest is ten now. And I was watching her pack up her schoolbag, and I thought about you. You were about her age the first time you came to my office."

"That's it?"

She laughed. "Okay, I thought I'd like it if Emma turned out to be a little like you."

"Just a little," I replied, laughing too.

I remembered my last session with Anne during college. I told her I wanted to be a therapist and work with troubled girls, like myself. At the end of that session, Anne had told me she was moving to Vermont in September because her husband had gotten a teaching position there.

I'd noticed that Anne was expecting when I first walked in but hadn't said anything.

"And you're having a baby."

Anne had reddened and touched her stomach. "I didn't know I was showing yet."

"To me you are. Congratulations. It's a lucky baby."

Ten years after that final meeting, Anne was saying she'd be happy for her daughter to be a little like me. I could sense her gap-toothed smile over the phone.

"Truth be told, Jamie, you taught me a lot of lessons about growing up. You were one hell of a teacher."

"Thank you, Anne, for everything."

"You're welcome. For what do I deserve the honor of this call?"

I thought about telling her that David was home, or that I'd met the Dalai Lama. I didn't want to tell her that I'd swallowed a bottle of sleeping pills. That would have been a therapy session. It was something else I wanted her to know. "I'm working with pregnant teens."

"How is that?"

"It's nice to be able to help them. It makes me happy to see the girls get their lives together. But I should go back to school soon, actually become a therapist. There's a thought."

"Hmm. Sounds like a good thought."

"I tamed my wolf. She's more of a companionable dog now."

Anne stayed quiet a moment. I imagined her lips pressed together, her tiny nod of acceptance. "Then you're in charge of you."

"I'm going to be alright." Saying this out loud to Anne, I knew it to be true. "Thanks for telling me what you were thinking this morning with Emma."

"My pleasure. Bye, Jamie."

"Bye, Anne."

I'D MET SALAM through his baking, because he was a pastry chef with a new book. And in keeping with this essential part of himself, Salam's body began to reject all food that wasn't sweets. Shortly thereafter, his body denied desserts as well. And then even oxygen seemed to offend his lungs, and he stopped taking in enough air.

Salam was admitted to St. Vincent's Hospital. A cuff around his forearm took his blood pressure every fifteen minutes, beeping a warning and tightening of its own accord. I read the fluctuating numbers to him. We learned the right amount of pressure for his blood to move through his veins and what was dangerously low. His vision occasionally darkened, his head falling back on the pillow.

"I'd be fainting now," he said, "if I were doing anything but lying in bed."

Sure enough, the next reading came in at half his usual pressure. The mystery of the real work of the heart became something ordinary.

A nurse showed me how to place the oxygen mask that hung behind his bed over his nose and turn the valve until we heard the rush of pure air. I adjusted the green elastic straps and the clear plastic cup over his nose and mouth, and then the only place I could kiss was his forehead.

An IV bag of fluids continuously hydrated him. He managed to eat and drink a little on his own. But another thing we learned was that the body stops needing food in the end. On his second morning in the hospital, I stood in the hallway with Chitra. She told me she had spoken with both their families. They all agreed that Salam should not travel to India in his condition. They'd waited too long. He'd grown too ill. He would spend his last days in New York.

By the third day of his hospitalization, our routine was set. I took time off from work. I'd arrive at St. Vincent's each morning at eight. Chitra would arrive a couple hours later, pushing the door of his room open with her shoulder, her hands full with a covered basket of food she had cooked. She usually caught us laughing. Laughter was our most common expression. It didn't need cause or reason; laughter was just the natural product of our overfull hearts. Surprisingly, Chitra often laughed with us too.

At lunch time, Chitra would spread the red tablecloth from home across the foot of the bed, then she'd unpack the various components of the meal. On a china plate from home, she'd create a colorful palette with a spoonful of each dish she'd cooked. Her final ritual was to tuck one purple and white orchid flower on the side of Salam's plate.

Even though Salam could eat only a bite of the curried chicken, lamb tikka, or whatever dishes she'd labored over, he loved the sight and smell of the food. He would enthusiastically praise the home-cooked meal. He enjoyed himself, no matter that the food was for smelling and admiring, was a symbol of life, more than it was for sustenance.

Chitra and I ate. After serving him, she would pull out two additional plates from the picnic basket, and make up plates for us. With our chairs pulled close to either side of Salam's bed, he was our table. We entertained him with small talk. His little harem pleased him. His eyes glowed with happiness as he listened to us talk and watched us enjoy the daily meal.

That room, Chitra and I, the taste and smell of Indian cooking, and even the administrations of the nurses, residents, and doctors became the whole world for Salam during his final week. He lost curiosity about what lay beyond his four walls. His room had one large window, with a view of Seventh Avenue in the West Village. Salam liked the plentiful sunlight that poured through that window, but on our trips back and forth to the bathroom, he never paused there to take in the view of the outside world. He was narrowing. The opposite of the growing and expanding that is typical for someone of his age. He was becoming smaller in every respect, until his world would wink out like the last bit of sun setting on the horizon.

During those days of frozen time, when the world outside Salam's hospital room didn't exist, and didn't require either of us to be in it, we enjoyed each occasion for him to fight his way out from the white sheets and place his thin feet on the floor to walk. He slung one arm around my shoulder, I clasped his waist—no bigger than my own—and we sidled to the bathroom, laughing for no reason other than the pleasure of standing upright together, because of how rare that had become, and knowing each "walk" we took could be his last.

I, by contrast, frequently took breaks from Salam's bedside while he slept. I'd peer down on Seventh Avenue and watch the world. I was outside of life and keenly aware of not needing to be anywhere except in that room, but I needed that world to continue being there, promising to go on. And when I left the hospital each evening, I drank in the cold night air, the brush of strangers on the sidewalk, the sounds of car horns and unknown voices.

Toward the end of the week, Chitra arrived a little later than usual, shocking me by having brought David. Salam was under the sheets in his hospital gown. I lay on the bed beside him, fully dressed, resting my head on his shoulder.

"Hi!" I sat up with surprise.

"Hi," Salam said, echoing me, seeming pleased to have a new visitor.

"I hope it's okay I came to see you," David said to Salam.

Chitra bent down and kissed Salam's cheek. "I brought lunch for all four of us. How are you feeling?"

"Great, starving." His hunger was not a lie, but it was not for food, it was for life that was still his to take, the last of everything. At times, I imagined I saw things exactly as Salam did: moments, objects, sensations, and words all had auras around them, flaunting their specificity and beauty and their finality. *This is the last lunch you will enjoy with friends, the last silver teaspoon you will dip in chutney, the last feel of another man's stubble brushing your cheek.*

That hospital-bed picnic was one of the best afternoons I ever had. And yet it never escaped my mind, or anyone else's, I think, that death was waiting for Salam. When David said goodbye, he kissed him on both cheeks. Stillness came over the room. A final parting was taking place; we all saw that. I imagined that David was making silent blessings for Salam's journey and rebirth.

In the final days, Salam and I continued to laugh, to caress each other's arms, to talk about the most mundane or meaningful of subjects of our lives with enjoyment and sorrow both. Old stories of his grandmother's kitchen and of David's and my secret language of twins unfurled quietly into the room, only for each other's ears.

Our walks stopped when Salam was given a catheter. Wordlessly, we both observed that he'd stood on his own feet for the last time without our knowing it. Then he was bed-bound, and suddenly there was pain. He was wracked with it. The cancer grabbed each bone and filled it with venom. He cried out, "My shins, they're crushing. My spine's caught afire." Cancer's poetry poured out of him.

That afternoon, the doctor came in and examined Salam.

"It's time to start administering morphine. Where is his wife? We will need her consent. You will all want to say your goodbyes because he will sleep until the end."

The doctor said this right over Salam's head, standing on the opposite side of the bed from where I sat. Outrage bloomed in my chest, and then just as quickly popped like a soap bubble from a child's wand. The words landed on Salam's ears comfortingly. He closed his eyes, almost imperceptibly relieved. This was what he'd been readying himself for. His task would be sleeping until the end. He accepted his final work.

"She just stepped out."

When Chitra returned an hour later, I told her I'd take a walk around the neighborhood and come back later if that was okay with her. We both understood we were now facing our goodbyes with Salam.

Standing on the sidewalk in front of the hospital, I didn't know where to go. It was winter and already nightfall. Fear gripped me. Wherever I went for the next couple hours, the same truth remained. I would return to this curb, enter this lobby, ride the elevator to the third floor, enter Salam's room, and say goodbye to him in words. I had never considered that there would be the gruesome opportunity to have a final conversation with him. I wiped frightened tears from my eyes and began walking south.

The walking was the beginning of the many hours, over many months, that I spent taking in what the Dalai Lama said to me. *Practice dying. This death is my own smaller death.*

As I walked, I imagined the top of my head opening. Clouds and blue sky tumbled through my open mind and plowed the previously untouched earth of my brain, aerating my whole being. Ignorance and pain and fear tumbled out of my mind. These things dropped off like pebbles falling off a flatbed truck as it rolled along. The craters these discarded emotions left behind were filled with the wisdom of letting go and being filled with the joy of giving.

I would lose Salam. He would depart this planet perhaps many, many years before I would. But if I could let him go, then maybe Salam being free of this world, free of his earthly body, would allow him to be with me always. Allow me to hold him in my mind, carried in my dreams, a spark of passion forever lit.

I reentered Salam's room nearly three hours later. Chitra was seated in a chair by his side. Salam's face looked so restful that I feared they had already administered morphine—that he was already in his final sleep.

Chitra must have read my mind. "The morphine will start tonight. He's just sleeping," she whispered. "Come outside with me."

We walked about ten paces from his room.

"I don't know how he fell asleep now. He was groaning with pain, and then he just shut his eyes. His face went smooth." I saw Chitra's fear for the first time.

I pressed the heels of my hands against my eyes, creating dots and squiggles behind my eyelids.

"I guess the end is here," Chitra said. "I don't think he should see either of us fall apart. He's doing so well with what he has to do."

I looked into Chitra's face; her normally shiny ink-black hair was dulled by the hospital's stale air. Her eyes, perhaps the prettiest feature in a face that contained all prettiness, were so sad. I closed my eyes and thought of David—helpless to stop himself from kissing her—making a fool of himself for her.

"What are you smiling about?"

I looked at her again. "Am I? I was thinking of you bringing David here to see Salam. I'm glad you did that. I wouldn't have."

A smile played across her face too. "You're welcome."

"Chitra, I'm so sorry for your loss, and that you had to share it with me. I'm sorry for everything."

Chitra gave me a good long look. "Jamila, I lied to you. When I came to your apartment that time and told you to leave Salam alone...you collapsed before I could leave. You weren't breathing, and I was scared that I'd be caught and blamed somehow. I gave you mouth-to-mouth resuscitation and you started breathing again and coughing and you threw up. Then I saw what you'd done."

"I threw up the pills."

"Yes. I rolled you on your side and I left."

"You saved my life. And you never told Salam what I'd done?"

She lowered her voice. "You took those pills out of passion. Salam leaving you was like losing your life, your reason to live. I envy that."

I turned toward Salam's door but Chitra took my arm. "Salam and I have the sanctity of our marriage. We have something that is more binding, but not that . . . to want to die without each other."

She'd saved me from myself and had the courage to speak to me with pure honesty on the day Salam would die. I felt she deserved the whole truth about me, the truth Salam would never hear.

"Chitra, this wasn't the first time. I've struggled with self-harm and suicide almost my whole life."

She looked at me anew, like I was, yet again, more foreign than she could comprehend.

"You and Salam have shared more than he and I have," I continued. "There's no comparison."

A second passed, and then we hugged for the very first time. Our embrace was mutual. It felt good to hold her. She was part of Salam, and maybe already part of David, and I hoped that she could be part of me too. Eventually, we loosened our arms and stepped back from each other.

Without another word, I walked back to the door of Salam's room.

I carefully sat on his bed and stroked his neck.

Salam opened his eyes. "Jamila. You're back."

"Are you in pain?"

"Yes. My spine has burning coals in it. He held up his hands, which were no longer tan in color, but gray and so much smaller, like my own. "Even these ache." Salam tilted his head so his face touched my hand that rested on his pillow. "You're chilly. Were you outside?"

"Yes, I took a walk."

Salam closed his eyes again. "Tell me where you went."

I spoke quietly. "I walked about a mile before even noticing where I was. I'd made my way down Broadway and then I saw I was heading right into Ground Zero. It's all lit up with spotlights. They're working, even at night."

Salam's eyes scanned my face briefly. He shifted onto his side to face me, wincing as he moved. "Go on."

"I watched the cranes and those trucks that pick up things."

"Grabbers," Salam said without opening his eyes.

"Yes, like prehistoric animals reaching out their big square heads to close their gnashing teeth around objects. I guess they're working below street level, laying foundations, the subway . . . all that rebuilding." I grew self-conscious. What were Salam and I going to say in these final moments?

After a while he noticed my silence. "Angel, it's easier to keep my eyes shut. If you talk, I can forget how much it hurts."

"Okay." I thought that idle chatter was no good, but I would keep talking. "I haven't told you much about meeting the Dalai Lama."

"You haven't."

"Can I lie down beside you?"

Salam smiled. "Give me a second here, no fast moves." He rolled onto his back again and tugged his body a few inches upright and onto the far side of the bed. He lifted his arm closest to me. "Okay, angel, get in here under my wing."

I curled into him, and before he closed his eyes again we kissed, a light, soft close-mouthed kiss. Salam's lips were as dry as paper. For the first time, he did not smell and taste of baking spices or bread, or mint toothpaste or coffee, but something sour. I didn't mind at all. It was the last.

"I've tried, but I can't come up with a better word than *holy* to describe him. When we first stood face-to-face, I found myself in tears."

Were these the words? Was this our goodbye? We were well into the night, and on that night Salam would be given morphine for his pain. The rest would be a vigil. How many words were left? I caught myself in the act. It was okay. No word was wrong; no word was right. Our total was already in place. Salam and I were already what we were. And that moment, so heavy with expectation and the pressure to correctly capture us, was freed.

Salam didn't say *go on*. But I knew from his breathing and the feel of his body that he was awake, waiting and listening still.

"I'm already using what he gave me—acceptance . . . and carrying on."

Salam stroked my arm. "Jamila, remember what I wrote in your book the night we met?"

"Yes. 'Jamila, please.'"

He let out a small cry that punctured the air. "You did it all. That 'please' contained everything I hoped for, like a birthday wish that is for perfect happiness, everything you long for in one wish. You did it all."

Chapter 14

David

I WAITED IN the inner office to see His Holiness, curious about his meeting with Jamie the day before. Our trip to Shambhala Center in Boulder, where the Dalai Lama would deliver teachings to a few thousand American students, was a week away. I'd had no time alone with him since the afternoon he arrived, when he'd given me the cymbals. His message to me, etched into the iron, was still un-deciphered.

The Dalai Lama entered the room and sat in the armchair beside me.

His hands pressed together in prayer, he rubbed the underside of his chin with his fingertips.

"David, in the path of the bodhisattva, a path we share, all bodhisattvas aspire to Buddhahood for the benefit of all sentient beings."

This was something I understood from my first days in his presence under the giant oak tree in England, before I'd been accepted as his student.

"Remember, the bodhisattva"—he pointed at me and then pressed his hand over his own heart—"is striving to bring all beings to Buddhahood, not merely himself, or else he would be a mere practitioner. The duty to free others is what binds the bodhisattva."

The Dalai Lama knew precisely the painful sense of duty and failure I had experienced from just this, my failure to help Lobsang, who struck me as a brother from first sight, and my lifelong failure to ease Jamie's suffering, my own twin.

"The bodhisattva has that call of duty. And the Mahayanas say there are three kinds of bodhisattvas, three paths for the bodhisattva. You are aware of the three?"

I had been aware of the three paths since I was fourteen years old and had taken my vows in Dharamsala. Through the tall window behind His Holiness, I saw that it had begun to rain. A naked fear grew in me that he was asking because I wasn't on the path, on any path of the bodhisattva. My mind struggled to come more awake—*bodhicitta* mind.

"The King, the Boatman, and the Shepherd. Those are the three kinds of bodhisattvas." My voice sounded like a child, reminding me of the first time I sat with him in New York City. I was so small my feet didn't reach the floor.

The Dalai Lama nodded. "The Shepherd's way is that he aspires to delay his own enlightenment until all other sentient beings have achieved Buddhahood, and then after his flock has crossed the threshold, he will close the gate behind him, achieving Buddhahood last."

His Holiness pursed his lips, leaning forward and twisting in his seat to make eye contact with me, he dipped his chin, asking if that was understood.

I nodded.

He continued. "The Boatman, he aspires to achieve Buddhahood *with* all sentient beings, together."

I nodded again.

"And lastly the King-like bodhisattva, his way is that he aspires to inhabit Buddha as soon as possible. And then help sentient beings full-fledged in his enlightenment."

The Dalai Lama's gaze turned outward, his eyes fixed on a distant spot—his mind moving somewhere. I watched his face. He was returning to one of the first lessons he'd ever given to me, as a child. I had no idea why.

Abruptly, he turned his full focus on to me. "Now I am the Dalai Lama. We Tibetans only believe in the one path." He raised one finger. "King is the way of the bodhisattva. But understand, even if I believed in other ways, even if I could choose, I would be a King-like bodhisattva. Here in this world, born leaders must lead, or else no sentient beings stand a chance to get out of the burning house. I am the fourteenth Dalai Lama, and I will be the last."

Awake mind—*bodhicitta*—seized my brain. My head felt lit up with electricity and my heart beat too fast, pushing behind my ribs.

I think the Dalai Lama saw exactly the state he'd put me in.

"Perhaps I possess the consciousness of the previous thirteen Dalai Lama's, and perhaps it is the consciousness of the Buddha, but the next leader of Tibet, the next 'Dalai Lama' will not." His eyes flashed with a look I'd never seen before. His anger.

I shrank, afraid of His Holiness for the first time. Nothing had prepared me for the shock of hearing this. Tibetans considered His Holiness to be the Buddha himself. Many wicks, one flame. Each of the fourteen Dalai Lamas bore the same enlightened consciousness, and yes, it was the actual consciousness of Buddha. The Buddha walked the earth in this man. Tibetan culture hinged on this tradition more than any other, that the true Dalai Lama, the enlightened, chosen child who bore this consciousness, could and would be found—after the death of the previous Dalai Lama.

"Your Holiness, forgive me," I stammered, "but how would Tibet go on without a Dalai Lama?"

"Tibet will have a Dalai Lama, the only person fit to rule the kingdom, after I am gone."

"I don't understand."

"You understood when you were ten years old. In England, you said to me that the Dalai Lama was like an acorn and an oak, always here in one form of life or another."

The Dalai Lama stood and went to the window. He looked out for a long time. When he faced me again, his face was stern.

"Tibetan doctrine holds that Buddha remains in the world forever, in the physical form of the Dalai Lama, a six-century-old tradition. I do not disagree that Tibet and the world need Buddha."

The Dalai Lama smiled, but his smile was not a happy one.

"Even if, after my death, the holiest monks within my lineage were capable of finding the innocent child who bears the enlightened consciousness of the Buddha, there is no one capable of holding reign over Tibet under relentless fire, while this innocent child becomes a effective leader So there is no point in delay. I myself will find the next great leader among my people. I myself will prepare him, and he will lead the Tibetan people as soon as I cannot. He will be the next King bodhisattva. If I do not do this, China will do it. They will elect their Dalai Lama, who will be a suffering puppet. And the innocent child who my highest monks, in their esteemed wisdom, find to bear my same consciousness, will disappear. I will make this change because I am now King bodhisattva. I am now Buddha! Here"—he pointed to the floor—"we need a lion in the kingdom. Here! This bodhisattva"—he struck his chest with his hand—"is the lion in the kingdom!"

Before my very eyes, a lion flexed and expanded his chest. The small room was filled by this awakened beast with his huge head and thick, flowing mane, his ancient face. He peered at me with his all-knowing amber eyes. He looked about to pounce. His twitching paws were nimble and deadly quick. I defensively raised my arms around my head.

"Now we have *bodhicitta* mind!" the Dalai Lama roared. In a single stride, he reached me and took my whole head in his grip. A lion's embrace. I trembled under his touch. Out of a womb-like darkness, His Holiness' face emerged once again.

He settled again in the chair beside me, breathing heavily. "David, now I'm asking you what kind of bodhisattva are you? You are not Tibetan, and you have a choice."

To speak just then was impossible. I wiped away tears I hadn't known were there.

Finally, I stammered, "Your Holiness, I believe I am a Boatman. My purpose is to cross the waters of *samsara*, to leave the waters of suffering, with all beings by my side, as the Boatman who guides the boat."

My throat constricted with the awesome amount of responsibility and desire I felt.

The Dalai Lama moved his chair in front of mine, so we sat facing each other. His lips were pressed together and he emitted a low hum.

"Here's what I want to tell you, David. You are a King who wants to be a Boatman. There is no choice but to become enlightened as soon as possible. You were born a *tulku*. You found me, came to me. I ask this of you now because I have made a discovery—each of us is needed here"—he pointed to the floor beneath us—"to do his or her job in this world without delays. If enlightenment, if wisdom, looms before you, you must grab it and use it. No matter who you leave behind."

I understood that the here and now he was speaking of was right outside that holy room, in the human and earthly place that was my home, New York City, a burning home of eight million who were unaware it was burning.

CHITRA AND I sat far apart on her couch, having just returned from Salam's hospital room. I was fairly certain I'd never see Salam again. I had a flight to Boulder in the morning and would be away for a little over a week. Salam didn't have a little over a week.

It was dusk, and the room had grown dark around us. I smelled the cinnamon tea from our steaming mugs on the table. A woman singing in Hindi played from the stereo speakers, sounding like water running through stones.

"Will you return to Mumbai?" I asked.

Chitra looked at me and sighed. I had not said, "After he dies," but we both knew that's what I meant.

"Yes. I'll buy a ticket right after he's gone."

When Chitra moved, I could smell the apple scent of her hair.

"Chitra, I owe you an apology. I'm so ashamed about what I did outside the museum that day. It was disrespectful." I couldn't face her as I said this and I looked down at my feet on the floor.

"Worse than kissing me is saying that you're ashamed to have."

My head jerked up at these words. Chitra was teasing me, a small smirk on her face. My belly tightened.

"I'm not ashamed of it like that," I cried. "I wanted to kiss you. I still do."

She smiled fleetingly. "Salam told me about you before we met. Jamila's bodhisattva brother. I was curious about you from the day you two showed up here. Remember? You and I sat on this couch and talked." She glanced around the room. "I trusted you immediately."

"I didn't deserve that trust."

"Why?" Now Chitra wore a look of surprise.

"I was here under false pretenses. I told myself that I came to New York because Jamie needed me, but her needing me rescued me from some deep trouble in Tibet. Before I came to New York, I was quite lost. Perhaps I still am."

"And Jamila was too." Chitra reached for her mug and took a sip of tea before responding. "You know what's weird? The day I went to see Jamila, to tell her to leave Salam alone, I trusted her too. I trusted her intentions, despite myself."

Listening to Chitra, I literally felt my heart. It physically ached, and I understood that expression for the first time.

"Then Jamila collapsed. I kneeled beside her, unsure what to do. And I thought of Salam. I thought *this is Salam's best friend in the world.* It was almost like I was his instrument. His will drove me to put my mouth to hers."

She shook her head, reflecting on her own peculiar actions.

I rose unsteadily to my feet, finding the lion and the king from deep inside me. Terrified, I found my new mantra. No delays. Here. Now.

"Come here, Chitra," I croaked.

She rose from the couch too and stood in front of me. I held tight to her. Against her back, my hands fell into her hair. It was silky and cool to the touch, and I wanted to keep my hands there forever.

"I want you to be okay. To be happy again one day."

Chitra began crying as I held her.

In my head I said *I love you.* And then I sensed so strongly that she had heard me and accepted it that I found the lion's courage to say it aloud.

"I love you, Chitra."

Her body went still and then became heavier in my arms, like a baby falling asleep. I felt her let the words in. She embraced me tighter.

FOUR OF US took the same flight to Boulder. Longo and I were seated several rows in front of the Dalai Lama and his personal assistant, Tenzin Geyche Tethong. I'd brought the gift His Holiness had given me, the cymbals, in my carry-on. They made a suspicious shape in the metal detectors at security but were permitted on board after I showed them to the TSA employee. I pulled the box from my backpack and began translating each syllabic character into English. Slowly, the Tibetan alphabet floated back to the surface of my mind, and I looked up the words that eluded me in the Tibetan/English dictionary I carried with me since my trip to Sichuan. Before we'd reached Boulder, I'd translated the inscription on the pad in front of me.

For David,
Our world is a pair of twins, suffering and enlightenment,
forever holding hands. One will never exist without
the other. Embrace them. See suffering with bodhicitta
mind. Spread Dharma wisdom with your whole being.

His Holiness had these made for me while I was missing from the Kirti Monastery in Tibet. That was before he'd met Jamie, and before I'd told him about her attempted suicide. I couldn't even remember the last time we'd discussed that I am a twin. It was an uncanny coincidence that he'd used the word twins. The suffering he referred to was Tibet, was Lobsang himself. The suffering His Holiness had hoped I'd see and ease was the suffering of Tibet. Yet precisely because I am a twin, I saw Lobsang with a twin's heart, I wanted to be united with him, and thus I grew blind to the hills around me, and even blind to his anguish.

I placed the cymbals over my eyes and my thoughts drifted. I was transported back to my first day in Sichuan Province. This time the arid world of the Himalayas shone crystal-clear before me. Tiny yellow, red, and white Yarrow flowers in full bloom swayed on their spindly stalks. Hornbills pierced the air with their yodeling cries and cast their shadows in flight over the Tibetans who walked the dusty roads, their wares on their backs, their children boomeranging back and away, back and away. I smelt the frying pumpkin seeds of the street-side kiosks, I tasted dumplings and barley tea again on my lips, but this time with bodhicitta mind. And when I met Lobsang in my mind's eye. I asked him how he was. If there was anything another student of Kirti, of Dharma could do for him. I saw him, and not an empty space inside me that he might fill.

When I surfaced from this vision and removed the cymbals from my face, I felt a presence beside me. I lifted my fingers to my face, convinced I felt the silk and weight of Chitra's hair running through them. And at my back, permanently reinforcing my very being, was Jamie, forever my twin in our present world of each of our making, in the womb of waiting and the tunnel of rebirth we traveled together and arrived in the same place, suffering and enlightenment, with clasped hands.

I opened my eyes. Longo was reading in the seat beside me. His hair was closely shorn, and his face clean-shaven and peaceful.

He turned to look at me. "You fell asleep."

"No. Did I tell you I've fallen in love?"

"With yourself again?"

This was the Longo of our shared past, who teased or ignored me. I laughed. "No. Her name is Chitra."

"She must be a saint."

"Yes, a saint and a sentient being."

"I'm happy for you. Being in love is a good thing to be."

"Yeah, I'm beginning to see that."

I pushed the pad of paper with the translation onto Longo's tray table. After reading it, he studied me with a long and steady gaze, then tugged my short ponytail the way the Dalai Lama had. He picked up the pencil and wrote on the bottom of the sheet of paper.

HHXIVDL FOREVER.

I laughed again. "Sorry if this is too earnest for you, but I'm glad we both ended up here, in New York, and on this plane."

"You have donkey breath." Longo smiled, picked up the book he was reading, and returned his attention to it.

I peered down the aisle for a glimpse of the Dalai Lama where he was partially visible between the seats. He waved.

"I'm gonna go thank him."

Longo rose to let me out of my seat. He thumped me on the back as I headed toward the back of the plane.

When he saw me approaching, Tenzin Geyche stood and moved down the aisle, allowing me access to the Dalai Lama.

"May I join you a moment?" I asked His Holiness.

He patted the seat beside him with both hands, as though I were a doggie he was trying to lure onto the seat.

"I just translated these." I held up the cymbals. "Thank you very much."

The Dalai Lama clasped my hand across the armrest. "So, now what are you thinking?"

If I do not examine my own defects, though outwardly a Dharma practitioner, I may act contrary to the Dharma. Therefore, continuously to examine my own faults and give them up is the practice of a bodhisattva.

I imagined steering a small boat with Jamie on board with me, leaving behind the waters of samsara. And yet, I'd never asked her to give up her suffering. I'd never built a boat for two and sailed her into safer waters. Just as quickly, I was struck by the memory of pushing Lobsang's wheelchair over the curb, forcing myself on him, and my relentless desire to bring him back to the Dharma. There was no bodhisattva in these moments, boatman or otherwise.

"Whenever I've seen pain and suffering in the world, I've seen myself in opposition to it. Like I could counter suffering with my Dharma wisdom. Not a compassionate, empathetic yin-yang, not seeing that there's a part of each in the heart of the other, but a polarity—fighting each other. I've never succeeded at easing others, at being a bodhisattva, because I've always thought suffering and enlightenment were opposites."

The Dalai Lama touched his finger to the end of his nose. "Bingo."

"That's what happened in Tibet. I grew so attached to Lobsang, or the idea of him, of me saving him, that I lost the path before me. I am lost in *samsara* with everyone else."

The Dalai Lama leaned back into his seat and made a little whistle through his teeth. "The whole world is one river. We're all in it."

His Holiness drew his hand away from me and folded both hands in his lap. With his eyes shut, his breathing slowed, and he appeared to fall asleep.

His eyes popped open again. "I've made a mistake about you, David. When you were a child, I saw a bodhisattva in you, but I missed that you are also a twin. And how do twins operate? Not one before the other. In the river of life, the waters of samsara, the Dharma is your paddle. As you have told me, you are to paddle your boat with others who are suffering within it, make your way toward enlightenment together."

All of the moments in my life when I'd recited my vows to myself again and again, seeking and searching for their wisdom, I'd been deaf and blind to their actual meaning. The memorization and the recitation are nothing. Just knowing my bodhisattva vow and not living it is like a boatman holding an oar, but never dipping it into the water, never paddling.

I rose to my feet and bowed again to my great teacher. From his seat, the Dalai Lama bowed his head back at me.

Epilogue

Jamila

THERE WERE TWO deaths that taught me what I had never gotten right about life—to live it.

Bethany called me one morning at home before I left for work. She'd never called me before.

"Jamila? I can't get her to eat or drink. A body can go without food, but she's got to drink."

"I'll come right over."

She needs straws, I thought, as my train crossed the Manhattan Bridge, the sun sparkling on the water. I thought of juice boxes with tiny straws.

When I arrived, Grandma sat at the kitchen table in her nightgown, her shoulders hunched. I'd kicked the legs of that same table many an evening waiting for Grandma to finish cooking my dinner. Now she sat there, the petulant child, with her bobbed hair and pink nightgown.

"It tastes so good," Grandma murmured, while sipping the green tea I'd brought. I held the box to her mouth, feeling proud that Grandma drank the entire thing. My arrival had resulted in her ingesting precious life-giving fluids.

But when she was done, she clutched her stomach and ran-hobbled to the bathroom. I stood outside the bathroom door and listened to her retch, feeling foolish for thinking I'd helped.

My mom got an appointment, and I took Grandma to her doctor's office the next day, where she underwent a series of tests, including a full-body scan after ingesting a sixteen-ounce can of barium. Worst of all was the doctor telling me she didn't like Grandma's aura.

A week later we knew that Grandma had advanced stomach cancer.

When I arrived at Grandma's that evening, Bethany whispered to me, "See if you can help her take a shower. She hasn't bathed in days."

Grandma liked the idea. I eased her out of her nightgown and underwear. Holding her by the arm while she carefully stepped over the tub, I thought *this is my future body.*

The warm water revived her. She turned her face into the stream, letting it run over her face and in her mouth. She held out her cupped hand for some shampoo. I kept the curtain open and held onto her tiny frame while she washed in case she slipped. I handed her a moistened toothbrush with toothpaste on it, and while the warm water washed over her body she brushed her teeth for the last time.

I wrapped her in a towel and rubbed her limbs through the thin terry-cloth to help dry her.

"Grandma, let's lotion you up."

While she sat naked on the edge of her bed, I smoothed lotion on her arms, her back, her thighs, and her feet. She was now too tender for massage. I remembered Salam's words from two years earlier: "My spine's caught afire."

I handed her the large plastic comb for her hair. Without the aid of a mirror, she made a perfect part down the middle and combed her hair down over each ear and straight down the back, the bangs over her forehead.

"Ah, I'm clean," she murmured. "There are new pajamas from your mother in my bottom drawer. Maybe I'll wear them." Grandma smiled as though we would be sharing a special treat.

The pajamas were white cotton, with tiny red flowers, a short-sleeve top that buttoned up the front. She was fresh as a hibiscus flower.

I settled Grandma on the couch, arranging her pillows and laying a cotton quilt over her, I tucked it around her legs. While she slept, I stroked her feet through the quilt.

My mother had been coming over every day directly from her last client. I found myself anxiously waiting for her. When she arrived, she kissed Grandma's forehead.

Grandma stirred. "Margot, you're here." She managed a smile for her daughter.

"Yes, I'm here. Rest."

Grandma obediently shut her eyes again.

My mom motioned for me to follow her to Grandma's bedroom. She took from the top dresser drawer a small brown bottle.

"The visiting nurse gave this to me . . . its morphine."

The nurse had shown Mom how to give the liquid morphine from a dropper, by mouth. She said only a few drops, but much more was allowed if the pain was bad.

"I need to warn you, Jamie. The morphine could put Grandma into a coma until she passes away."

"I know how it works. Please, Mom, it's not time yet."

My mom put the bottle back.

"We'll decide together, Jamie. There's no rush."

Mom sat beside me on Grandma's bed and wrapped her arms around my body. I let my head rest on her shoulder. She stroked my back slowly, the sort of comforting I was used to only from Grandma herself.

When it was time for Bethany to leave for the day she said, "This is it . . . my goodbye. She won't be here day after tomorrow."

Bethany hugged me and then my mother goodbye. She bent at the waist, hovering over Grandma where she lay on the couch, and peered meaningfully into her face. I had to smile, remembering Grandma's remarks about Bethany's stature. She was built like a professional baseball player.

"Lill, it's been an honor to know you. Have a safe passage. I'll see you one day in heaven."

I stifled a sob, grateful for Bethany's belief, even though I didn't, couldn't share it.

She gave Grandma a sad last glance that cut through me.

By nightfall Grandma was groaning incessantly with pain. She'd been tossing on the couch for hours, semi-consciously.

Then abruptly, she opened her eyes and looked right at us alertly. My mom and I were both kneeling on the floor beside the couch and she looked directly at each of us and said, "My girls." She went back to sleep, looking slightly more peaceful. I thought of her story of Melody, her stillborn daughter, her conviction that she had two baby girls all along.

In the middle of the night, Grandma began writhing in pain while she slept.

"Your father's coming first thing in the morning. Should we wait until then to start the morphine? I can't stand seeing her pain."

"I'll go get it," I said.

I looked away while my mom fed her the morphine like a baby bird. Grandma's body knew to want it.

We were like her Will then, when he had waited in the same living room sixty years earlier for her to give birth to Melody. But this time, she was in the living room with us, and she was laboring to die. I sat on the floor by the couch and whispered to her in case she could hear. I told her about David and Chitra, that they were on their way.

When Grandma furrowed her brow and moaned in her sleep, my mom gave a couple drops more morphine. We passed the night sitting beside her.

The following morning, my father arrived. He took in the circumstances and disappeared into the apartment. He returned with a basin, soap, and washcloth.

"You two give her a sponge bath. There's a rattle starting."

"A rattle?"

"Her breathing."

I couldn't hear it yet. But I washed Grandma with Ivory soap and a worn white washcloth. I talked and talked. I told her to look for Salam, to play mah-jongg with him. Then Grandma was breathing as though she were jogging while she slept.

Mom said, "It's okay to let go, you can go."

The rattle grew unbelievably loud. Grandma's breath chugged like a train running over gravel. It was torture, but then she would take long breaks, too long, where she didn't inhale for five seconds, ten seconds, and then she would fight for air, sucking it in, showing us what real labor was.

My mother kept speaking to her.

"Ma, it's okay to die. You were a good mother, the best, and a wonderful grandmother. We love you so much. We're here with you. Let go, Ma."

My father sat guard in an armchair between Grandma and the front door, as though death would need to gain entry past him. He rose and approached Grandma.

"Lill, you carry on."

I cried and gripped Grandma's hand.

"Goodbye, Grandma," I whispered, barely able to speak.

Then Grandma opened her eyes. Raising her head off the pillow, she looked directly at me.

"Grandma, you're awake!" For a second, it seemed she might return to us, recovered.

Ever so slightly, she shook her head, *no,* reading my thoughts. Grandma lifted her hand and waved goodbye. She fell back on the pillow, her eyes full of tears. She lowered her eyes and the tears ran across her temples. The rattle stopped.

We had a few more hours to be with her before her body was picked up by the funeral home. I sat on the floor by the couch and continued to touch Grandma and prepare myself for her being taken away. I hadn't lingered as long with Salam's dead body. After the nurse had unplugged his machines, no longer needed, and smoothed the bed sheets around him, I had kissed his face, his cheeks, his forehead, his unresponsive lips, and I left him. Chitra remained with the body of her deceased husband—it was her right. I'd had the living one.

I had not wanted to physically embrace Salam's deceased body. With Grandma it was different. I wanted to consume the last remnants of her. I pressed my cheek to hers and placed her hand atop my head, the way Grandma had touched me a million times.

My mother held and hugged Grandma's inert body too. She told her, "You died with a lot of grace. You had a good death, Ma." It was true.

The men from the funeral home arrived. Their awkwardness made me think that not many people died at home on their couches these days. They hesitantly unzipped a long black body bag on the floor beside the couch. We backed away as they lifted Grandma and placed her in the unzipped bag, like so many suits in a hanging bag. I was overcome with crying again, with needing to say goodbye more. I kneeled on the floor and put my face against hers one last time.

"Bye for now, Grandma," I whispered finally.

HOURS AFTER THEY take Grandma's body away, I hug my parents goodbye and leave her apartment. I walk through lower Manhattan directionless. It's a beautiful night for walking and for brushing shoulders with strangers.

Eventually, I look up to see that I am in front of the Strand Bookstore where I first met Salam. Its windows pour light onto the wide sidewalk, a beacon in a city of night owls, walkers, and yet unmet lovers. I enter the store and go directly to the cookbook aisle where I'd first spoken to Salam. The white spine of a book leaps out at me from the shelf. SWEETS OF PANJAB: DESSERTS FROM AN INDIAN HOME. With one finger, I tip the book off the shelf toward me and open its cover.

SALAM MIRRANI.

In all capitals, just as I remember it. This copy doesn't say, "To Jamila, please." With the tip of my finger, I trace the letters of his name. "Hi there. It's me." I turn the pages to the recipe for a Persimmon dessert, Chitra's recipe. I can taste the sugar melting on my tongue, like cotton candy. I close the book, kiss the cover and return it to its place. The lights of the bookstore all blink out at once. A soft cry of surprise rises from all around the store. I turn and look in to the vast unlit space, inhaling the unfamiliar peace of darkness.

I follow the surprised and excited voices through the store and out to the sidewalk. Never before have I stood anywhere in New York City and seen not a single light shining in the dark. My city is like a nighttime forest. I feel the presence of Grandma's raven-like trickery, her wink, her farewell. I feel Salam's hand in mine. I walk out into it, unafraid.

David

I WASN'T THERE in Salam's final hours, the beeping of machines, and then the silence when they were finally turned off. That was Chitra's and Jamie's experience to share. I saw Chitra one more time before she flew home to Mumbai. One more meeting where I dared again to tell her *I love you* and we shared a kiss that I can still remember thousands of kisses later.

I bought a one-way ticket to Lhasa, Tibet. From there, I boarded a tiny plane to Sichuan where I went directly to my old guest house and checked in to the same room for an undetermined period of time.

The following morning, I took a motorcycle cab to Lobsang's home. I brought with me a basket of fruit and no translator. I thought I'd just make my peace offering and leave. If Lobsang wanted to speak to me, ever, he could easily find the Westerner who was studying at Kirti.

I knocked on Lobsang's door and waited. This time, I wore a ski hat, a down jacket and a scarf Jamie had knitted for me. It was January and the Tibetans I saw everywhere were bundled up with many layers of hand-woven clothes. There was an air of desertion to the place. The curtains behind the thin glass windows were drawn. There was a thin undisturbed layer of dust on his doorstep.

A neighbor spoke behind my shoulder, startling me. I recognized him from my prior visit to Lobsang six months earlier.

"They're gone," he said, in Tibetan.

"They moved? Do you know where?"

"They're gone. No goodbyes. The place just emptied one day. I locked the door for them, but they won't be back."

I raised the fruit basket I'd brought for Lobsang. "Would you like this then?"

Eyeing the apples, chestnuts, walnuts, cherries, and apricots, he gave me a gap-toothed smile, the first, and took the basket.

I headed down the long road I'd walked so many times, this time I hailed a motorcycle cab to get back to my guest house.

The following day, I bought a second fruit basket for Gayto Rinpoche, the teacher the Dalai Lama had chosen for me at Kirti Monastery, and I walked the short road from my guest house to the monastery, for the first time entering its gates.

This time in Sichuan, I settled in and got to know Gayto Rinpoche. I felt the warmth and connection, and yes *bodhicitta* mind for learning that had evaded me completely when I'd come in the summer.

Each day, I walked between my guest house and the monastery and looked off into the distant steppes of the Tibetan Plateau. Last summer the hills were aflame in Himalayan poppies and Asian bleeding-hearts, yellow, maroon, and pink flowers. This time of year the alpine meadow grasslands were partially covered in snow. Patches of exposed grassland were spotted with grazing yak and the bare branches of walnut and chestnut trees.

Every afternoon, I visited the Internet café near my guest house and exchanged messages with Jamie and with Chitra. I frequently heard from my parents, and Longo too, and even received bright and quirky messages from Grandma.

Chitra was re-enrolled in her graduate program. She had closed up the Mumbai apartment she had shared with Salam and had moved into a new place with a friend. After two months of daily correspondence, we decided to meet in Dharamsala for a holiday together.

I told the Dalai Lama I was coming for a visit. He told me to come see him first thing. The McLeod Ganj and Namgyal Monastery, where His Holiness lives and practices, was a sight for sore eyes. I'd become a bodhisattva in these study rooms and found long stretches of Dharma peace breathing that air. I walked the traversing, uphill pathways with a heart full of joy. As always, there were monks and pilgrims at every turn on the many paths around the monastery. I found myself walking directly toward a child who tottered down the path, a Tibetan toddler on strong bowed legs, she stumbled toward me, shrieking with joy. Although I'd never seen a young child at the monastery, she felt oddly familiar. As I passed her mother on my way toward the Dalai Lama's rooms, she looked familiar too.

His Holiness pulled open his office door the moment I approached.

"Come in! Come see."

Together we went to the window that overlooked the lawns at the base of Namgyal Monastery, where fifteen years earlier Longo and I and the other students had watched monks playing soccer, their robes tucked into their belts, their legs slicing through the cool Himalayan air.

The view I saw was of a robin-egg blue sky, dotted with fluffy clouds. A group of hornbills flew east, too high above for me to hear their honking calls. My eyes were drawn to the now empty lawns, bordered with evergreen rhododendrons and dormant roses. Bent forward in an immediately recognizable posture, one ear to the ground, I could see Lobsang pruning back the rose bushes from his wheelchair.

"He could use a little help getting to know our different tree varieties here."

"He's here with you!" My heart soared with the hornbills.

"Yes, as a gardener, not a monk. He's married now." His Holiness winked playfully. "But I'd say his Dharma practice is as strong as the most learned monks still. After all, he's been touched by fire."

"He's left that burning house. The little girl on the path, and her mom, now I know why they looked familiar. That's his family?"

"Little Pema. She's a hoot. She's enrolled in the Tibetan school already, one year early."

I turned to my father-teacher with a smile. And then for the first time in our long relationship, I took parting of him first. "I'll be right back, I want to go say hello to Lobsang."

A FEW MONTHS later, I flew to Mumbai and met all of Chitra's family, including her grandma, who was much like my own. We had a simple wedding ceremony at sunset in the Indian Himalayas, officiated by the Dalai Lama. And we have a framed Jewish katuba that was signed weeks later in New York at a family party in my parents' apartment to celebrate our marriage.

That was the last time I saw Grandma. As we danced, she whispered in my ear, "You've found someone to walk with."

Chitra finished her master's degree in Persian language and literature, graduating with the first signs of the pregnancy showing under her gown. In the pictures, Chitra is leaning backward to make it show more, holding her rolled-up diploma against her stomach.

I LEAN OVER Chitra's giant lap to look out the window at the New York City skyline as we descend. We bought our tickets three days ago when Jamie called to say, "You'd better come now."

But as we changed planes in London, Jamie reached me to say Grandma had just passed away. I felt winded, a bottomless darkness.

"Jamie, I'm so close. I'm so sorry that I wasn't there."

"You were. Just bring yourselves back here safely."

"We're on our way."

"She waved goodbye to us, David."

I can see Grandma's crooked hand passing me one final salute.

In the air, it's a beautiful night. The lights of Manhattan are pixilated and clear against a black sky. The Chrysler Building and the Empire State Building are glowing beacons that tell me the world is still here. We gaze together out the window, my face half-buried in Chitra's hair. We feel the plane's nose pointing toward Earth.

Chitra says, "It's so beautiful." Her hand covers mine on the armrest.

And like a wink, the lights of the city go out. Disappear. The jewel box of a city has gone dark from shore to shore. We both gasp.

Chitra whispers, "What happened?"

We feel the plane hesitate, level out again. I wrap my arm around Chitra's belly.

The plane's descent begins again. The pilot's voice comes through the overhead speakers.

"Well, if you're looking out your window, you may have noticed that New York City has gone dark. A city-wide blackout. I've been told it's the first time since 1977. But JFK has its generators up and running, and I can see our landing strip just fine. Make sure your seat belts are fastened. We've been given clearance to land."

Then we are nothing but our waiting to land in the darkness, like a full-term baby in the womb, like the day my sister and I were born.

Rachel Stolzman Gullo is the author of *The Sign for Drowning* (Trumpeter, 2008). Her poetry and fiction have appeared in various publications. *Practice Dying* was a semi-finalist for Best Novel in the William Faulkner-William Wisdom Literary Competition, received a fellowship from Summer Literary Seminars, and was a finalist for the Inkubate Literary Blockbuster Challenge.

9 781945 805684